Pride Publishing books by Kristian Parker

Speak Its Name
To Light a Fire
Call it Love
Spotlight on Love

Village Affairs
The Rule of Three
Three's Company
Triple Intent

Two Tribes
Fool's Gold
Everything Changes

Collections
My Bloody Valentine: Venetian Valentine
Sun, Sea and Spotted Squid

Two Tribes

EVERYTHING CHANGES

KRISTIAN PARKER

Everything Changes
ISBN # 978-1-80250-524-5

Interior text design by Claire Siemaszkiewicz
Pride Publishing

Published in 2023 by Pride Publishing, United Kingdom.

Pride Publishing is an imprint of Totally Entwined Group Limited.

EVERYTHING CHANGES

Dedication

To Julia, thank you for being wonderful all these years. I am a lucky man to have you. xxx

Chapter One

A mechanical reindeer serenaded the city with a rendition of *Away in A Manger.* It was like a call to arms for crowds of people who flocked to Manchester's centre to stand out in the freezing cold, getting drunk on overpriced beer. All in the name of celebrating the festive period.

The smells of cinnamon and hot dogs competed as Shaun Moseley walked through the packed crowds. He had woken up to the wonder of Christmas late in life. His upbringing had been a long way from the perfect families he had watched with envy on the television. His mother thought good parenting had been to let them sit in the pub with her and her mates instead of leaving them at home. Shaun had preferred to stay at home. At least then his younger brother, Liam, could fall asleep in his own bed instead of a pub floor.

Even with those thoughts milling around in his head, the cheer bursting out of Manchester this drizzly afternoon was infectious. He got his mobile phone out of his jacket and dialled.

"If you're ringing to tell me we're not having curry for dinner tonight, I'm going to be upset."

Typical of Liam. No hello or anything. Straight to what he'd be fed that night. He didn't deserve to be so slim.

"Have no fear, I've already made it," Shaun grumbled. "Bloody hell, do you always think with your stomach?"

"No," Liam replied with a laugh. "Ask Marco."

"Shut up. How gross."

"You're only jealous."

Talk about an understatement. "Too bloody right I am," Shaun muttered. "Three months without any action is like being in lockdown all over again. It's not natural."

"It must be hard," Liam said before collapsing into hysterics at his own joke.

"Hilarious," Shaun replied drily.

He walked deeper into the markets. It might have only been midday but already people were the worse for wear. Manchester had earned a reputation for hard partying many decades ago and the city still wore it as a badge of honour. It gave Shaun a strange sense of pride in his birth town. After being away for years, he had enjoyed spending the last few months here. Well, on the outskirts, but he took trips into town whenever he could.

The stalls were packed with things. Food, cooking implements and, for some reason, bird tables. Shaun could just imagine a husband leaving his Christmas gift shopping until the last minute and panic-buying one.

He had no idea how one of those things would be wrapped.

"So, what did you want? Not to ask about my sex life, I'm sure," Liam continued.

"Nothing much. I'm in the markets and it made me feel all Christmassy," Shaun replied. He stopped and examined a stuffed robin in a waistcoat. Who on earth would buy that?

"It's bloody weeks away yet," Liam moaned. "I haven't even thought what to get Marco. It's a bit hard when he won't let me out of his sight."

He had a point. Ever since Liam had been released from hospital after being shot by crime boss Jonny Wellingham, Liam's boyfriend Marco Ponti hadn't let him move without being by his side. That would drive Shaun mad, but Liam was in love and lapped it up.

Careful, Shaun, you're beginning to sound like a jaded old queen.

"They've invented a new thing, little brother," Shaun said. "It's called the internet. I'll show you when I get home. It's brilliant."

"Funny guy," Liam replied. "You're as bad as him, anyway. You've only been gone an hour and you're checking up on me."

Bored of the stuffed animals, Shaun moved on to a stall that had a revolutionary garlic press whose sign proclaimed he'd been living half a life without. Shaun examined it and wasn't sure that was strictly true. He'd managed for over thirty years without this essential piece of kit. He had an inkling he could struggle on for the rest.

"Actually, it wasn't about you, believe it or not. I wanted to talk to you about Christmas," he said. "I might go home to Blackpool. It would be nice to see some of the guys." Silence on the other end of the line told him what Liam thought of that idea. "Liam? Are you still there?"

"You know you can't," Liam said quietly. "Marco said it isn't safe yet."

Shaun slammed the garlic press back down onto the stall.

"Breakages are paid for," said the stall holder.

It was hard to take someone seriously who had garlic bulb earrings with a matching necklace.

"Sorry," he mouthed to her. But the ever-present frustration had risen up in him. "Fuck's sake, Liam. It's been three months. Wellingham is probably on the Costa del Knobhead, drinking sangria or something."

Liam sighed. "Until their uncle comes and gets things properly running, you can't. It won't be for much longer. Besides—"

"Besides what?" Shaun snapped.

"I thought it might be nice for us to spend it together," Liam said shyly. "It's been years."

A flash of guilt replaced the anger. They hadn't had Christmas together since Shaun had left Manchester many years ago. He'd been travelling too much. Then when he went to Blackpool, Liam had taken up with Wellingham's gang and couldn't be persuaded to come to his. Shaun had found it hard to tempt him to a nut roast in a yoga bed and breakfast when Jonny offered drink, drugs and God knew what in a mansion.

"I suppose I'm cooking the dinner as well, am I?" Shaun asked.

"It will give you something to think about," Liam answered. "You love planning shit like this. Remember your thirtieth? You choreographed your own surprise party."

Shaun couldn't deny it. He didn't like to leave things to chance. "So we'll all sit around eating turkey and Christmas pud?" he asked.

"Don't forget the crackers."

"Like one big happy family, eh?"

"You could make an effort, seeing as it's Christmas," Liam offered.

"I will talk to you, Dolly and Claire," Shaun said haughtily. "Maybe Marco if he doesn't keep banging on about being a big gangster."

"Fine, whatever," Liam said.

Shaun could hear himself being mean—a frequent occurrence since he'd been caught up in this whole nightmare. Staying by Liam's bedside those awful days in the hospital, he'd vowed to take better care of his brother. Now he was being childish because he couldn't go to his mates at Christmas. They still thought he was looking after Liam so it wasn't like they even expected him.

"Well, I suppose I'd better get the rest of my shopping done. I thought I'd do those homemade naans you like."

"Ace. I'll tell Marco, he loves them. Oh and, Shaun..."

"What now?" Shaun laughed. "You're very needy today, Li."

"Remember that fudge stall on Brazenose Street? I wonder if it's still there."

When their mother would spend the afternoon in the pub, she would give them a ten-pound note to spend on the markets. Shaun would always go straight for chocolate, but Liam plumped for as much fudge as he could buy. Then he would nibble his collection every day to make it last. Of course, Shaun's chocolate would be gone before the Queen made her speech.

"I reckon it will be," Shaun said with a smile.

"Pretty please," Liam begged.

Shaun sighed. "You soft lad. It's miles back the way I've just come from."

"Pretty please with cherries on top?"

How could he refuse him? Liam had missed out on so much in his short life and even though Wellingham's bullet had nearly killed him, he was happier than Shaun had ever seen him.

"Fine, seeing as it's you," Shaun said. "But I get to choose the flavours. You always had weird shit like cherry fizz or lemon meringue."

"I only did that to keep you off them," Liam confided.

"Crafty little shit."

Shaun set off the way he had just been. In doing so, he walked straight into an incredibly good-looking young man behind him. But that wasn't what made Shaun jump. Keeping as calm as possible, he pushed past and set off towards the edge of the market, his heart racing.

"I'll let you go then," Liam said with a chuckle.

"Wait," Shaun said, unease flooding his system. "I don't know if I'm being paranoid, but I think someone's following me."

"What? Tell me what you mean," Liam said. All traces of amusement had left Liam's voice.

"This guy. I saw him in Marks and Spencer and in the food market. Now I've just headed back to that bloody fudge stall and he's there. Right behind me."

"Are you sure it's the same person?" Liam replied.

"Course I am. He's gorgeous. I never forget a fit lad. Like I said, I'm probably just being paranoid. Manchester isn't all that big."

He wasn't sure if his mind was playing tricks on him, but it felt like the crowds had become denser. Office workers still in their formal clothes but with flashing antlers on their heads shouted to one another over the din. Shaun wanted to fight his way to the street now. He glanced back and to his horror, the guy wasn't far behind him.

"Okay, I'm not being paranoid. He's following me. Absolutely sure of it," he whispered. He half expected a hand to grab his shoulder at any moment. He might be surrounded by people, but Shaun could hardly beg a stranger for help.

"Act natural. I'll dial Marco in," Liam said.

Shaun wanted to run, but they had rehearsed this so many times he remembered what Marco had drilled into him. *Don't give away that you know. If you panic, they will panic, then things can get out of hand.*

With every bit of his self-control, he walked slowly past the little wooden chalets selling their wares as though he were browsing like anyone else.

"Shaun?"

Marco Ponti had the thickest Italian accent to go with his brooding good looks. If he hadn't been an ambitious gangster who'd nearly got them killed, Shaun would have been happy for his brother. But now Shaun needed his confidence and knowledge.

"What do I do?" Shaun replied.

"Stay calm. Can you get a photo?" Marco asked.

Shaun frantically scanned the markets. He saw a man dressed as an elf, giving out free chocolates. He dashed over.

"Any chance of a pic?" he asked him. "My brother is after an outfit like this for Christmas morning. I said I'd make him one."

The man nodded and Shaun made a big fuss of positioning himself to get the selfie absolutely perfect. He managed to get the mysterious figure in one of them and sent it off to Marco.

"You have a happy Christmas," Shaun said to the elf and carried on towards the street.

He tried to work out the best escape routes out of the city. He'd got the train in from the little village near their old farmhouse hideout. The last thing he wanted was to lead any would-be attackers there. He had to lose them somehow.

"Did you get it?" he asked.

"Just looking," Liam said. "Shit, fuck. It's Deano."

Terror gripped Shaun. Deano was the worst of Wellingham's henchmen. He'd hated Liam when they had both been in the gang together. Him along with the rest of Wellingham's Boys had been on the missing list ever since Marco had burned Jonny's pool house to the ground. Shaun had been sure that Jonny would cut his losses and leave town. He'd been wrong.

"Okay, Claire has been on to Giovanni and Enzo. Giovanni is miles away, but Enzo is only in Moston. He'll be at Aldi in Ancoats in twenty minutes. Can you get there?"

Enzo and Giovanni were Marco's muscle-bound cousins. Exceptionally handsome but constantly preoccupied with pumping iron, Shaun had given them a wide berth ever since they'd arrived.

"Ancoats is fucking miles away."

"I know, but if he comes any farther in, he'll get caught up in traffic. Can you do it?" Marco asked.

Shaun glanced around again. Every young man could be a potential attacker.

"I'm scared, Marco," he said quietly.

"Listen to me. You have to keep up the pretence. You're just on a shopping trip. Laugh."

"What?"

"Laugh. I've just told you the best joke ever. You have no cares in the world. Fucking laugh."

Shaun did as he was told, he wouldn't have won an award for his performance, but it would do. "I'm nearly at the street. Then what?"

"Stop and browse at the stall next to you. You're in no rush, remember."

Shaun found himself showing an interest in an apple-shaped wine cooler. The hopeful stall holder approached.

"Once I get to the street, what do I do?" Shaun asked, ignoring the man who seemed determined to impress him with a demonstration on how to get the top of the cooler off.

"Get to the Northern Quarter," Liam said. "It'll be crowded."

A bead of sweat trickled down Shaun's back even though the December air had chilled him all day.

"I'm not cut out for this. I don't think I can—"

Panic rose within him. He'd been sure he wouldn't be affected by this life. He'd refused to have anything to do with their dodgy deals ever since Liam, Marco and the others had turned up on his doorstep in Blackpool. Shaun had accused Marco of being paranoid for making him stay with them all these weeks. He'd only done it so Liam would focus on getting well again.

"Shaun," Marco barked down the phone. "You have no choice. Get yourself ready. Swallow it down and do everything I tell you."

Shaun tried to control his panic and fought the temptation to lay into Marco. None of them would be in this position if he'd just done what his uncle said and waited for reinforcements from Italy. Instead, he'd taken it upon himself to try and ruin Jonny Wellingham. That had resulted in Liam taking a bullet and Shaun being trapped with the rest of them. Jonny evidently did see him as a target and now he needed Marco to get him out of there alive. "Okay, ready," he managed.

"Then go."

Shaun wandered to the edge of the market. Crowds were spilling out onto the pavements and tired security guards kept telling them to get back in with their drinks. Shaun desperately wanted to throw himself on their mercy and beg for help, but that would only cause bigger issues further down the line. He had no appetite for being labelled a grass on top of everything else.

"Tell Enzo he'd better bloody be there," Shaun said.

"He will be, and I'll be on the other end of the phone all the time. You can do this, Shaun," Marco coaxed.

Summoning all this inner strength, Shaun stepped out of the seemingly safe confines of the markets. He'd been on the pavement mere seconds when a car roared up from a side street. It screeched to a halt metres from where he stood.

To his horror, Deano grabbed hold of his arm and hauled him towards the car. Shaun heard Marco calling his name down the phone, but it all happened so quickly.

The rear door of the car opened, and Jonny Wellingham's long-time deputy, Harry, glared at him from the back. There were no prizes for guessing who would be at the other end of this joyride. If he got in that vehicle, his life might very well be over.

Then the rage built within him. He would not die like this. He had escaped these bastards once in his life. He would do it again.

There were plenty of people around to witness what was going on. Surely he could use that to his advantage. Then a sharp stab of pain stung in his side, telling him that this Deano had a knife to him.

"If you say anything, I'll stick you," Deano whispered in his ear.

But Shaun wasn't going to be scared that easily. "Help," he screamed. "This man is trying to rob me. He's got a knife."

The security who had been dealing with unruly drinkers spun around. A young couple stood open-mouthed.

Deano slapped him on the shoulder. "Come on, Shaun. These people won't know you're joking. Sorry, he gets a bit confused when he's had one too many."

To Shaun's relief, Deano released his grip ever so slightly.

"Get him in the fucking car," Harry shouted.

Deano jabbed the knife harder.

Shaun didn't fancy bleeding to death while day trippers took selfies with him. "Help me," he screamed. Shaun wriggled out of Deano's clutches, exposing the knife. A woman screamed when she saw it.

The security guards were approaching at speed now. Shaun could see one talking into his headset. He prayed it would be to the police. Deano pulled the blade away from him. Relief flooded through Shaun's body, making his legs turn to jelly. But now wasn't the time to lose it, not when he was a long way from safety.

Two lads were getting out of the car, but before they could do anything, Shaun shoved Deano with all his might. He fell against a handmade candle stall. The stall tipped over, sending hundreds of candles in all the colours of the rainbow rolling along the floor. The stallholder shouted and grabbed hold of Deano, who was trying to get up. Shaun saw his opportunity.

He ran as fast as his legs would carry him out of the markets and into the main shopping streets of the city. When he reached the corner, he glanced back to see lads scrambling out of the car. One hollered when they saw him.

The chase of Shaun's life was on.

Chapter Two

Shaun ran into the pedestrians-only street. They would have to follow him on foot, which would give him a fighting chance.

As he ran past a buzzing restaurant, he searched his pockets for his phone but couldn't find it anywhere. In the pandemonium at the market, he must have dropped it. Panic gripped him. He was on his own and would have to rely on Enzo being at the meeting point when he got there.

Voices were shouting behind him. It had been too much to hope that they would have given up. But now things were on a more level playing field, he felt a glimmer of confidence. *You can do this, just bloody focus.*

Dashing through a narrow alleyway, he came out on Market Street. It was known as one of the busiest shopping streets in Europe, and today was no exception. Shoppers were jostling each other to get to the next stop on their gift-buying plan. As far as cover went, he couldn't hope for better.

Snaking through a gang of women, he headed towards one of the bigger department stores. There would be cameras everywhere, which could work in his favour.

Trying his best not to draw too much attention to himself, he half walked, half ran through the doors of Primark, the huge store that dominated the corner of Market Street and Piccadilly Gardens. He needed to buy himself some time. It would be no good if he got to the meeting place and had to stand, totally exposed, while he waited for Enzo. He had to try to lose Deano and his mates.

Grabbing the first thing that came to hand, he found a shop assistant. "Where are the fitting rooms?" he panted.

She gave him a strange stare but pointed him to the corner of the store. "Over there."

Glancing over at the door he had come through showed him Deano and another lad bursting into the shop. They looked around but hadn't seen him yet. He raced over to where the assistant had pointed.

Suddenly he realised he had hold of a frilly gingham blouse. *Good old Manchester for not judging.* The changing rooms were relatively empty. The woman at the entrance yelped as he barged past the short queue.

"Hey!" she shouted.

"Sorry, it's an emergency," Shaun replied. He went into the cubicle and tugged the curtain closed.

The figure that greeted him in the mirror was not a pretty one. Covered in sweat with his hair all over the place, he needed to calm down if he was going to survive this. He was still nowhere near the supermarket where Enzo would be waiting. Leaning against the wall, he let his breathing slow. The winding streets of the Northern Quarter were not far away. Once there, he could keep his head down far easier.

With a heartbeat that sounded like the latest house music track, he crept out of the changing room. Deano stood perilously close, checking every aisle. Thankfully, a display of hideous Christmas jumpers was blocking his eyeline. Shaun crouched down and readied himself to make a run for it.

"Was it any good? Seeing as it was an emergency."

He turned to the changing room attendant who stared at him expectantly.

"What?" he asked.

"The top? Was it worth pushing your way through?"

Shaun handed it to her. "No, not my colour."

Breaking cover, he made it to the exit in record time. With his route plotted in his mind, he focused solely on the task at hand.

Back out on the street, it had begun to pour down. *Nice one, Manchester. You never miss a chance to rain.*

"Fucking great," Shaun muttered to himself as he made his way through people wrestling with umbrellas and putting plastic wrappers over pushchairs. A boarded-up department store lay on the other side of the street, and he kept as close to its side as possible.

At least the rain had fixed the wild curls that started to sag and get in his eyes. He could be anyone sheltering from the sudden weather, and so allowed himself to break into a run.

Once on the edge of the Northern Quarter, he looked behind him. Deano and his accomplice were following him at breakneck speed. They must have seen him in Primark. Did these twats never give up? He knew what would happen to them if they did. Jonny Wellingham didn't have a reputation as a forgiving man.

The bars of Manchester were doing a roaring trade. Cheesy Christmas tunes filled his ears as he dodged the unsteady punters congregating outside, smoking. He could do this. He was smarter and fitter than his two pursuers. Liam had told him Deano was the most ambitious in the gang, but those delusions of grandeur made him sloppy. Shaun could work with that.

Two women came out of one of the bars. One of them muttered and put up her umbrella. Shaun launched towards her and grabbed it.

"What the fuck?"

"I need this more than you," Shaun replied.

Before she could respond, he put it up and ran towards an alley that led to the next street. Enjoying the cover for a moment, he took a second to plan his next move. Long streets led up to Ancoats. He would be exposed, but he only had minutes now until Enzo would be in position. *Speed over stealth,* he told himself.

The wind had picked up and he struggled to keep the umbrella under control. Thankfully, he made it through to the next street and sprinted past the trendy shops. First a barbers, then a gay bookshop, then a real ale bar. Everyone inside having a nice, relaxing day. Totally unaware that he was running for his life. His thighs were screaming in protest but the adrenaline coursing through his system made it bearable.

He couldn't see anyone following him and ditched the stupid, cheap umbrella that kept turning inside out. Right at that moment, a shout sounded, making him run faster. He'd dumped it too soon.

The people around him were thinning out now as they took shelter from the Manchester weather. If he made it up this street, he would be on Ancoats, a big circular road that imprisoned the city centre. The sign for the supermarket towered over the smaller shops. He hardly dared to think he'd nearly made it. He couldn't let up now.

Ironically, as he ran past Manchester Police Museum, a young lad in a hoodie appeared from the side of a building. He blocked the pavement and the knife he held glinted under the streetlights. He must have been waiting for Shaun. Using all his strength, Shaun launched his body at the lad and they both fell to the floor in a mass of tangled limbs. Totally aware that this opponent would have no issues with sticking that knife in him, Shaun had to get free.

Employing the yoga flexibility he'd spent years perfecting, he dodged the lad's hands and once he got to his feet, aimed a well-placed kick to his stomach. The lad groaned and doubled over in pain. Satisfied that he'd winded him, Shaun set off again.

Now he had to worry about all angles, not just behind him. Of course Wellingham would be managing the whole thing from wherever he was hiding his saggy old arse. Shaun could just imagine him barking orders into his phone. Then he thought how terrified Liam would be that his phone had gone dead. He absolutely had to get to Enzo. Once in the car, he could tell Liam he had made it.

The rain pelted him hard now and made his curls drip into his eyes. He shoved them out of the way and sprinted. The tussle with Jonny's hired muscle had given him some much-needed determination. Panic still threatened to overwhelm him, but he pushed it as far down as possible. It would come, but not yet, not until it was safe.

As usual, Ancoats was a major traffic jam. Shaun glanced from car to car. Any of them could have Harry or someone else in them. Reaching into his pocket, he pushed his keys between each finger, creating a rudimentary knuckleduster. If a car door opened, he would be ready.

The long road held mainly commercial properties, so there were hardly any people on the pavements. This gave him absolutely no cover. Then, to his horror, he saw two lads standing outside one of Jonny's brothels from back in the day when he'd had girls working for him. Was that their hideout? Had Shaun inadvertently delivered himself to Wellingham?

Thank God. They hadn't seen him yet.

Not daring to move, he let his heart rate return to normal and tried to think how to get past the old brothel and to safety.

"You on the run?" came a voice.

He whirled around and saw a homeless man in an abandoned shop doorway, watching him. "You could say that, but not from the police," he replied.

"Ooh. Not a gangster, are you?" the man said. The smirk he gave Shaun told him he thought that idea highly amusing.

Shaun shook his head. "You wouldn't believe me if I told you. Let's just say I'm fucked if I don't get to Aldi in five minutes and I could do with not being recognised."

The homeless man rifled in his rucksack and produced a yellow poncho from inside. "You wouldn't believe how many of these I get given," he said. "It's yours."

Shaun pulled it over his head. It clung to his wet hair and he tried his best not to rip it. It covered his distinctive Hilfiger jacket and his soaking-wet curls.

Digging in his pocket, he found a wad of notes. He handed them all to the man who had quite possibly saved his life. "Do something good with it, yeah?" he said.

Without waiting for a reply, he took a deep breath and ran towards the meeting spot.

This is the last push. You've got this.

Staying on the other side of the road and keeping the hood close to his face, he hoped he wouldn't be seen. The lads outside the brothel seemed more interested in their phones than trying to find him, the days when Wellingham gang members were on top of their game seemingly over.

His heart danced when he saw the Audi A3 double-parked near the doors of the supermarket.

He yanked the door open and leapt in. Enzo instinctively reached for what Shaun presumed was a gun then relaxed when he saw Shaun's flushed face.

"Get me the fuck out of here," Shaun shouted, fighting to control his breath.

Enzo fired the car into life and they sped out of the car park. In the safety of the car, Shaun allowed his body to relax. Then the waves of realisation of what had just happened hit him. He started to shake uncontrollably.

"I think I'm going to be sick," he shouted.

Enzo flicked the window down. They were stuck in the traffic Shaun had just run past.

"Go up that street," Shaun managed. He gulped in a lungful of air, but it stank of petrol and fumes. It made him all the more certain he could throw up at any minute.

Enzo steered the car into a narrow street. Lined with what had once been imposing cotton mills that the city of Manchester had sprung up around, they now housed huge apartments with even bigger price tags.

Enzo stopped the car. Shaun scrambled out and threw up against a wall. He held on to the cold brick as though it were the only thing keeping him upright.

When his body had nothing else to give, he shakily stood, wiped his mouth with his sleeve and made his way back to the car. It took all his strength to pull the door open. He slumped back into the passenger seat.

"You don't look so good," Enzo said. He rifled in the glove compartment and handed Shaun a tissue.

"I don't feel it," Shaun replied. Mortified that his breath stank of the remnants of his lunch, he took the tissue and wiped his mouth. He stole a glance at Enzo. His kind face told Shaun that he was safe.

"Are you ready?" Enzo asked, the glimmer of a smile dancing across his face.

"Yes," Shaun replied. "And thank you."

"All in a day's work." Enzo grinned.

It was too soon for jokes, but Shaun had no appetite for an argument.

"Then bloody floor it," Shaun muttered. "I'm never coming into this city again as long as I live. Which, if you people have anything to do with it, won't be very long."

Enzo raised an eyebrow but didn't reply. Instead they sped off up the narrow alleyway and towards home.

Chapter Three

His stomach had finally settled now they were on the way out of the city. He still had the bright yellow poncho on, which made him sweat. He ripped the plastic monstrosity off him and threw it in the back of the car. "What a bag of shite that is. I'm still soaked," he grumbled.

Enzo leant forward and turned the heating up.

Spinning around in his seat, Shaun tried to see out of the rear window. He couldn't shake the fear that they were being followed.

"There is no one after us," Enzo said. "I can guarantee that."

"How do you know that? Do you have superhuman gangster powers or something?"

"There is no one in the rear-view mirror."

Fear gave way to rage. Shaun hadn't asked for this life. It had been forced upon him by his stupid brother falling into bed with an Italian mobster. He never thought he would see the day when he pined for Blackpool.

"Are you still cold?" Enzo asked.

"I'm sweating like a bastard," Shaun spat back. He leant forward and turned the dial down.

Enzo ignored the attitude radiating from Shaun and punched some buttons on the phone that sat in a holster on the dash.

"Enzo?" Marco's voice boomed from the speakers of the car.

"I've got him," Enzo said.

Marco breathed a sigh of relief. "Liam. He's got him."

"Shaun?" Liam asked, clearly grabbing the phone from his lover.

"I'm safe," Shaun said. "Just."

"Oh thank God," Liam said. "Shaun, I'm so sorry, I—"

"Can we just leave all that shit until I get home?" Shaun demanded. He couldn't bear to listen to the apologies just yet. He'd had to listen to Marco trying to get his absolution every night when he'd returned to the farm from sitting with Liam in the hospital and had no appetite for it right now. It astounded him that these people acted as though they didn't have a choice. Everyone had a choice. Except for him. He'd been dragged into this situation against his will and found himself in a trap that, try as he might, he couldn't escape from.

"Hurry home," Liam said.

Home? What a joke.

"We will," Enzo said. "I've got to do something first, but I wanted you to know he's safe. We'll be there as soon as possible, I promise."

Not waiting for a reply, Enzo terminated the call. They were in the suburbs of Manchester now. Shaun wondered if he would ever feel safe going into the centre of the city again. He resented everything from the last few months. "Are you kidnapping me now?" he snapped.

Enzo laughed. "Not quite. I've got a suggestion. You might appreciate it."

"If it's a memory wipe of the last hour, then you've got yourself a deal."

"You will be all right," Enzo said. "You have had a terrifying experience. Allow your body to calm. Breathe and let it happen."

The tears were building up inside Shaun. If he let go of his walls, would he ever stop crying? He had no idea how to process all this. "It's all right for you," he muttered. "You're used to all this shit. For some of us, being chased through the streets of Manchester is a bit unnerving."

Enzo remained silent but turned off the main road out of the city.

"Where are we going?" Shaun asked.

"I told you. I have an idea that will make you feel better. Trust me."

Shaun couldn't even raise the energy to ask any more questions. He hated being mean to Liam. He absolutely knew what his brother would be feeling—it would be the same as Shaun had felt when Marco had contacted him to say Liam had been shot. Coming the day after finding out his mother had been murdered by the same man, it had been the worst moment of his life. *Fucking Jonny Wellingham.* Shaun wished he'd never heard that name.

He'd never forget racing to Manchester Royal Infirmary where Claire had been waiting for him. Dashing through those corridors and trying to take in everything the doctor had said to him while just wanting to see his brother for himself. He'd seen countless movies with those scenes where the hospital corridor seems longer than The Great Wall of China. Now he could totally understand.

He made a mental note to try and be nicer to Liam and not take his stress out on him. He'd probably fail, but he would try.

Enzo drove for a little while longer, and Shaun continued to struggle to get his thoughts under control. He hadn't really taken Marco's worry about Jonny seriously. It sent chills through him that Wellingham's boys could have been following him for days or even weeks. He could slap Liam for dragging him into this whirlpool it seemed no one had any control over.

"Do you?" he asked eventually.

"Do I what?" Enzo replied, snapping to attention.

"Get used to it?"

Enzo sighed. "I believe in what I do," he said eventually.

They were on the moors now. The vast expanse of nature for miles around made it feel like they could be on top of the world. Enzo pulled onto a car park, stopping on the rough gravel that scrunched under the tyres. Silently, he cut the engine and turned to Shaun. "Go on then."

"Go on what?"

"Get some air. Good clean air."

Enzo reached across and opened the car door. Shaun was a slender, medium-sized man, but everything about Enzo was big. Towering over Shaun at easily six foot five, he had thickset muscles. He and his brother, Giovanni, had set up a weightlifting gym in the empty barn next to the farmhouse and spent most of their time in there, pumping up their muscles and reminiscing about their motherland of Italy. Shaun had heard them from his bedroom window when he'd spent another night alone watching television.

He hopped out of the car, slamming the door behind him, and strode out onto the moor. The rain lashed down with force up here, but his clothes were still sodden from the chase across town so he couldn't have cared less.

Enzo had been right though. Getting some big lungfuls of air did help to calm things inside. Inhaling it as though his life depended on it, Shaun did the relaxation exercises he'd learnt on his travels. *In through the nose and out through the mouth. Slowly does it.*

With it being a weekday, there wasn't a soul around. He wandered down the path a little. Some sheep scuttled away and into the undergrowth. In the distance, a reservoir lay nestled in the hillside. Over to his right, the Manchester skyline loomed in the distance and, even farther, the airport.

It all seemed a long way away. He stopped and took it all in. At last, calm seemed to return. He didn't fancy going back to the farm just yet though. A hundred questions would be waiting for him. All he really wanted to do was get under the duvet and forget today.

"I never get used to it."

Shaun almost jumped sky high when he realised Enzo had followed him. For a heavyset man, he didn't make much noise… No doubt a useful skill in his line of work. He was so much bigger than Shaun, and his jet-black hair and tan skin seemed at odds with the cold, damp day.

"Bloody hell," Shaun complained. "You nearly gave me a heart attack then."

They stood side by side, watching some birds flocking over the reservoir.

"When I was in a yoga retreat in Kathmandu, they had all sorts of gay-coloured birds," Shaun said. "All we have are shitty brown things."

He kicked a stone.

"I've seen you doing your yoga," Enzo said. "Did you learn it on your travels? You should come and do some weights with me and Giovanni. It would be far more beneficial than getting yourself into silly poses."

"Have you been perving over me then?"

Enzo reddened. "It's not a big house. You can't help it."

Shaun regretted his big mouth. Enzo had done something kind for him and he should make an effort not to shoot him down every time he tried to speak. They wandered a little farther down the path.

"It's weird to think that my whole childhood was spent in that place," Shaun said, nodding to Manchester in the distance. "Where did you grow up?"

"I grew up in Rome. Well, a little village about an hour out of the city. I was very lucky in a lot of ways, but…"

Shaun glanced at him. He found him difficult to read, but there was definite pain there.

"But what?"

"Being attracted to men was not part of that world. Not until Uncle Z came. He changed everyone's view."

Shaun whirled around. "You're gay?" he asked in astonishment.

Enzo raised an eyebrow. "Is it so surprising? Marco. Uncle Z."

"Bloody hell," Shaun said. "My gaydar is way out of sync."

"Perhaps if you'd spoken to me once in a while, you'd have had a better chance of figuring me out," Enzo said.

His words weren't spiteful but simply stating a fact. A fact Shaun couldn't even begin to deny. Embarrassment burnt over his skin. He had been behaving obstructively since coming to the farm. Now he could see himself through Enzo's eyes and he didn't like it. "Have I been such a bitch?" he ventured.

Enzo glanced over at him and winked. Shaun had noticed that Enzo was handsome—it was impossible not to. But he hadn't taken the time to see his dark brown eyes or the way they crinkled at the sides when he smiled. Whether it was the fact he'd just saved his life or something deeper, Shaun imagined staring into those eyes and losing himself.

"We should get back," he said. "I need to finish tonight's dinner. I know my place and I don't fancy being shouted at by Marco for not doing it."

"And there he goes," Enzo muttered. "Back into his shell. You would find this whole experience a damned sight easier if you were a little nicer to those around you. We are not all villains, you know."

Once again, a flash of rage blew through Shaun's system. He didn't want to be schooled in how to be a gangster. Not by anyone, no matter how deep their eyes were.

"Thank you for the advice on how to survive a fucking gang war that I want nothing to do with," he snapped. "I was terrified today, Enzo. Do you understand what that means? I can't just toe the line and chuckle while my brother or any of you go out there time and again. If I get to know you, like you, it just adds to my fears. I can't do it. I won't."

He was babbling now, but his mouth couldn't seem to stop. To his amazement, Enzo came over and wrapped his arms around him. Shaun fitted perfectly, his head nestling in the crook of Enzo's neck.

Enzo's strong arms instantly calmed him and the shivers he had been battling since he got in the car simply disappeared.

"I get terrified too," Enzo said softly.

"How do you stand it?"

"I have no idea. You're not the only one in the whirlpool, I suppose."

Shaun looked up just as Enzo stared down at him. Their lips were almost touching, but then reality hit Shaun like a sledgehammer. Having an affair with a gangster had put his brother in the hospital. He had no intention of spinning that particular bottle.

He broke away, trying to ignore the hurt on Enzo's face. "They'll be missing us now," he said, smoothing down his jacket.

Enzo nodded and they strolled to the car in silence. Once inside, Enzo handed him a chocolate bar. "Sugar is good too."

Shaun noted it was his favourite. Was this an accident? Now in the safety of the car again, he relaxed. Perhaps it wouldn't hurt to let people in a little. He had been lonely sitting in his room night after night. But he also didn't fancy being privy to everything they discussed. Just being in the farm would probably get him a prison stretch. If he turned a blind eye to crime being discussed, he would only be adding to that. But that wasn't Enzo's fault and Shaun needed to direct his anger at the right people in future.

"Thank you, Enzo. You've been very good to me today."

"You were in shock and that's not surprising. You are not of this world."

As Enzo set off out of the car park, Shaun laughed, despite himself. "You make me sound like a ghost."

Enzo chuckled too. "Not like that, but you weren't raised with fighting in your blood. I know you and Liam had a tough start, but we were taught to use brute force where words won't help."

Looking at the thick fingers gripping the steering wheel and muscular arms revealed by the shirt rolled up to his elbows, Shaun could well understand how facing Enzo in a fight would be a daunting business. "I am lucky that I have you and Giovanni to defend me when I need it then," he said quietly.

Enzo glanced at him. "Whatever it takes."

Shaun smiled and flicked the radio on. He stared out of the window at the moors and listened to the music, letting his body relax into safety once again.

"Don't go to sleep," Enzo said.

"Why not?"

"You need to remember everything for Marco. Let go properly after that."

Shaun shook his head. They were always thinking of the greater good. Enzo had been right. It had been ingrained in them from birth.

How the fuck have I got myself here?

Enzo turned the radio on and hummed softly to the tune that played. Thankful not to have the burden of conversation, Shaun stole a glance at Enzo. His strong profile and jawline gave Shaun the jitters. When he'd had his arms around him, Shaun had felt more protected than he had in a long time. Even before this nightmare had begun.

Enzo's huge hands gripped the steering wheel. He was a man totally in control. Shaun found himself imagining what it would be like to have those hands holding his body. Yet underneath it all, he sensed a more peaceful man.

With his resolve wavering, Shaun allowed himself to consider that maybe he had got this man all wrong. But what was he to do about it? That was something Shaun would have to give some thought to.

Chapter Four

"Is there anything else you've missed?" Marco said. He ran his hand through his hair. "No matter how small. You need to be sure, Shaun."

"No. Honestly, nothing," Shaun replied. He glanced at Enzo, who smiled kindly at him. "I kept it all in my bloody head so I could tell you. Don't have a go at me on top of everything else."

Liam placed his hand on Marco's arm. "Go easy, yeah?"

They were in the lounge of the farmhouse. Shaun sat in a chair by the old fireplace, across from Liam and Marco on the couch, and Enzo stood by the window. He had been restless ever since they'd returned. Liam had flung his arms around Shaun and barely left his side since they appeared at the door.

"I don't like it," Enzo said. "It's pretty aggressive for his first move."

Marco rubbed his face. "Fuck knows where the slimy bastard was. Typical of him to send bloody Harry to do his dirty work."

"And that wanker, Deano," Liam added.

Marco's face suddenly lit up. "Will you ring Claire? We need to double up security on the flats this weekend. Where's Dolly?"

Liam got up and glanced nervously at Shaun. "She said she would sort out dinner."

They all groaned. Dolly was the worst cook. Shaun had been doing the meals in an effort to earn his keep and had had to wrestle his apron from her on more than one occasion. The idea that she would be polluting the curry he'd spent most of the morning cooking filled him with horror.

"Well, that puts the full stop on my day of shit."

"I'll go and ring Claire," Liam said, leaving the room.

"Tell her to get me a McDonald's on her way home," Shaun shouted after him.

Enzo crossed the room and sat next to Marco. "What are we going to do? You want me and Giovanni to find the bastard? We can do it nice and clean."

As if on cue, Giovanni strode into the room. Slightly smaller than Enzo and three years older, he had that unmistakable twinkle in his eye that Shaun had only noticed today on Enzo.

"Find Wellingham?" Giovanni said. "Just follow the smell of Old Spice." He clapped his hand on Shaun's shoulder, making him jump. "Dolly told me what happened. Sounds like you aced it, but I'm sorry it happened to you."

Clumsy as they might be, Shaun appreciated Giovanni's words. He didn't feel that he deserved them though. Anyone would have done what he did. It wasn't as if he'd saved a kitten from a burning building. But he decided not to react with his usual smart mouth.

"Thank you, Giovanni. I'll be all right. Just a bit shaken up," he said, mustering a weak smile.

Marco, who had been lost in thought, sat up. "I'm not spending days trying to find him. He'll be all over the place. We need to lure him out."

"How?" Giovanni asked.

"Fuck knows," Marco said. "But there has to be a way."

"Seems to me that you harden the market against him," Shaun said. He had resolutely told himself he wouldn't get involved and there he went, firing out ideas, like he was on *The Gangster Apprentice.*

But he'd done it now. Marco, Enzo and Giovanni all stared at him.

"We do what?" Marco asked.

"Harden the market," Shaun said. "Sell your drugs at cost. As for the girls, just make enough to pay them. Don't worry about your profit. Even if he gets some shit off the back of a lorry, he'll never be able to compete."

Marco thought about it for a second and grinned. "I like it. We don't need Manchester's fucking money anyway. Not yet. Uncle Z wants all of it, not some. If we slash prices, no one will touch that old dinosaur."

"Precisely," Shaun said. He hated to admit it, but he did enjoy the admiring glances the three handsome Italian men were flashing in his direction.

"I'm sorry for all of this, Shaun," Marco said. "Truly I am, but I have to protect us all. You understand?"

Shaun nodded. "Yeah. It would be cute if your uncle could speed up the reinforcements though. I suddenly feel less safe."

This fabled Uncle Z had spent the last three months finding new men. They had lost most of their gang in an ambush in Naples earlier in the year. Shaun got the feeling that Marco and his desperation to prove to his uncle that he wasn't a lost cause had had a lot to do with it. That desperation had almost cost Liam his life. Perhaps Shaun would be better off being more involved. He didn't rate Marco's ability for leadership all that highly.

"Are you going to contact Uncle?" Enzo asked.

Marco nodded. "Already done it."

The mysterious Uncle Z lurked on the periphery, giving out orders and paying for everything. It gave Shaun the creeps. He didn't like his life being controlled by someone he'd never even met.

"What does he have to say?" Shaun said, unsuccessfully trying to keep the sarcasm out of his voice. Marco bristled. They all acted as though he were some kind of god.

"He says that you will have to have a bodyguard from now on," Marco informed him.

"A what?" Shaun yelped.

"This isn't up for discussion," Marco said firmly.

"And who exactly will be assigned to this role?" Shaun continued.

Marco looked at Enzo. "You will."

Enzo nodded. "Fine, whatever."

Anger flooded Shaun's system once more. "And I have no say in this, I presume."

"No, Shaun," Marco said. "You don't. Enzo put himself at risk getting you out of there today. I'm not doing that again."

Shaun had no desire to be in the same room as these toxic males any longer. He stood and walked over to the door. "This is getting fucking ridiculous. I didn't ask for any of it."

He hated being this childish, but the frustration made him react like this. He felt a stranger in his own skin these days, either crying or raging. It was exhausting and he hated it.

"Where are you going?" Marco asked.

"Don't worry, I'm not daring to leave your prison compound," Shaun fired back. "Is it permissible to try and coax Dolly into not completely ruining the curry I slaved over for you ungrateful bastards?"

"Shaun, Marco is only trying to help," Enzo interjected.

"It would have helped if he had left me the fuck alone in the first place," Shaun shouted over his shoulder as he marched out of the room. He let the door bang behind him like the sulky teenager he was rapidly regressing into.

He made his way into the kitchen and instantly winced as the smell of overcooked meat hit him. Dolly busied herself chopping a carrot.

"Hello, love," she said. "I had a taste of that curry and it's a bit hot for me. Shepherd's pie tonight instead. I've put your curry in the freezer."

He couldn't even argue. It would serve them all right to eat this shit. Perhaps then they'd appreciate him a bit more. So he nodded and slumped down at the table.

"Still a bit shaken up?" Dolly continued.

"I guess," Shaun replied. "Today's been hard."

She finished chopping and threw the little orange shards into the pan. Shaun bit his tongue to stop from commenting. With a decent slug of ketchup on it, even Dolly's cooking could be rescued.

"It won't help taking it out on all and sundry, you know," Dolly said.

He liked Dolly. Ever since he'd arrived at the farm after being told he wasn't safe at home in Blackpool, she'd been the one he had gravitated towards. He got on with Claire, but she and Liam were as thick as thieves. She'd tell Marco everything he said. Not that he feared bloody Marco.

The truth in her words gave them a sharp edge that Shaun knew he couldn't defend himself against. Being in the wrong was another situation he despised with a passion.

"I hate this, Doll," Shaun said. Tiredness made him crave to be under the duvet upstairs. "I wish—"

"Wishing is a pointless activity unless you're going to make it happen. I learnt that years ago, love," she interrupted. "It doesn't do to focus on what you don't have."

"Like freedom, you mean?"

Dolly peered into the pan and stirred it. "Do you think I had much choice when Claire turned up at my door? Of course, I could have sent them away, but your brother would probably be floating upside down in the canal by now."

Shaun stared at her. She had kept herself in decent shape over the years. Her platinum-blonde hair was swept up in a twist and he had never seen her without a full face of makeup on. He liked her.

"I didn't really think about that," he said quietly.

Dropping the wooden spoon on the kitchen surface and making Shaun shudder, Dolly picked up the bag of potatoes and sat next to him. "You've been so busy pushing against this, you haven't thought about much else. If you don't mind me saying," she countered.

Other than his room and the kitchen, Shaun hadn't spent a great deal of time with anyone else in the farmhouse. Raised voices rang through from the lounge, but the sound was too muffled to be able to work out what was being said. He suspected he was the topic of conversation.

Dolly started to peel a potato. To Shaun's horror, she didn't put down newspaper on the table he'd spent his days scrubbing. But even he didn't dare to mention it at that moment. "You're always so calm," he said instead. "How do you do it?"

She stopped peeling and thought for a second. "I don't expect anything. Three months ago, I thought I saw the path for the rest of my life. Living in my little flat and keeping a few punters on for my retirement."

Dolly had been one of the most successful sex workers in Manchester. She had easily made the transition to madam, but Jonny had sacked her after he declared her past her sell-by date. Since coming to the farm, she had thrived. Giving guidance to Claire on how to run the girls and fussing around Marco and Liam had brought out a side to her that even she said she didn't recognise.

Shaun wished he could be more like her. "Don't you care that they trashed your whole life? Wellingham ruined everything in your home. I don't understand why you aren't raging."

"Not everything," she said. "When Giovanni took me home, I got my photos and mother's ashes. Anything else… What does it really matter in the end? It's just things."

Shaun tidied some of the crap that had been left on the table. He saw Enzo's car keys with the big flag of Italy keyring. "Did you know Enzo is gay?"

"There's a lot of it about," Dolly said with a chuckle.

"I'll bloody say," Shaun replied. "My gaydar was completely off."

Dolly frowned at him. "Maybe that's because you've made fuck-all effort since they arrived."

Shaun pulled a face. "I've had a near-death experience today, thank you. How about the lecture waits until tomorrow?"

They had definitely nearly kissed at the reservoir. Shaun wondered what it would be like to kiss Enzo, with his full lips and chiselled jawline. Something had awoken in him and it was not a good sign. He didn't need any more complications in his life. The minute he got the word, he would be out of here. A romantic entanglement would screw that right up.

Getting up from the table, he glanced out of the window. The rolling hills led down to a valley filled with trees. From the other side of the house, the Manchester skyline could just about be made out. Shaun liked the fact that this side of the house had nothing to do with that bloody city.

He had a handful of good memories of Manchester, but mostly the city represented dealing with his mother, avoiding her boyfriends and trying to give Liam whatever childhood he could manage. It didn't appear that this period of his life was going to produce much joy either. He meant what he'd said to Enzo. He would never set foot in that city again.

"Every time Liam goes out with them, I feel sick," he said. "I wish he'd never set eyes on any of them. I begged him not to join Jonny bloody Wellingham. I tried everything but he thought he was God's gift."

"You did your best for him, I'm sure," Dolly soothed.

"Fat lot of good it did either of us."

"Hey now, Liam is a wonderful lad. A lot of that is to do with you. Give yourself a break."

The clock that chimed with different birdsong filled the room with the noise of an owl. Dolly made a face. "That bloody clock."

Giovanni had sent off for it from an advert in a Sunday newspaper. He had decided it would make the place more homely. Instead, it drove everyone mad, but they hadn't the heart to get rid of it.

"He wants me to have protection when I go out," Shaun said. "Marco. Well, Uncle Z, but it's the same bloody thing."

Shrugging, Dolly carried on butchering the potato she had in her grip. "It's not a bad idea. Would you feel safe going out on your own anyway? After what's happened."

Shaun had been so focused on shooting the idea down he hadn't even thought how he would feel without Enzo by his side. "I certainly don't want a repeat of today. That's for sure."

"There you go then. Instead, you get a very handsome Italian stallion on your arm. You'll be the talk of the town. There are worse things that can happen to a person."

He did need to change his attitude. "Fine. Your pep talk has been successful. I'll make more of an effort," Shaun conceded. "I wish I could see the world like you do. I promise I'll try."

Dolly raised a glass of red wine from amongst her ingredients. "I'll drink to that."

"Hey, isn't that for the gravy?"

Taking a healthy glug, Dolly put the glass down. "I think a dish can have too many flavours, don't you? I want the meat to have a chance to shine."

Shaun took in the dry mince still sizzling away. It would take a miracle for that to have a starring role in anything but a cremation.

"New Shaun incoming. I'll try and think of something to do for everyone to show I'm not a complete bitch." He drained the rest of the wine from Dolly's glass

Dolly gave him her dazzling smile. "That's the spirit. If you could include Jonny Wellingham's head on a platter in that, I'm sure we'd all sleep a lot safer in our beds. I'm not ashamed to tell you, him being back on the scene gives me the jitters."

Shaun thought about it for a second. "I think Marco is right. If we lure him out into the open, we can force his hand. He's had three months to cook up whatever plans he has. All we have to do is work out what they are."

"We'll make a gangster of you yet," Dolly replied with her trademark cackle.

Chapter Five

Shaun sat in the lounge, trying to get the taste of Dolly's cooking out of his mouth with a large bag of M&Ms. The television blared out some nonsense featuring teams of people trying to rescue a ball from a tank of water while blindfolded.

Enzo came in and sat on the other end of the sofa. He was dressed in joggers and a hoodie. Shaun watched him as he got himself settled. Ever since the reservoir, he felt awkward around him. Had Enzo even felt the same as him? Or was Shaun just reading way too much into it because he was scared and looking for someone to latch on to?

"What the hell is this?" Enzo asked, frowning at the TV.

Shaun flicked the off button and silence overtook the room. "Some crap. Who knows?"

"Are you feeling calmer?" Enzo ventured.

He tried to remember Dolly's words from earlier. If the day had taught him anything, it was that he had to learn to direct his anger properly. To be mean to Enzo would be like kicking the family dog. Besides, he had saved his life. He owed him more than just backchat. He sighed and offered the bag to Enzo, who took a chocolate.

"I was out of line with Marco. I'll apologise to him," Shaun said. "I just feel so hemmed in here. You lot are all one team while I'm cleaning the lounge and peeling spuds."

"I realise that, but none of us want the situation to be like this," Enzo said. "Especially not Marco."

Shaun wasn't so sure about that. In the last three months that they had been thrown together, Marco had revelled in being the one in charge. To be fair, he had done a fairly good job and Shaun didn't want this to become personal. Judging by the way Marco and Liam's relationship had gone from strength to strength, a feud with Marco could make Shaun's life very uncomfortable indeed.

Giovanni came into the room. He helped himself to a chocolate and slumped down in the chair. "How is our little convict now?" he said. "You got over your hissy fit?"

"Don't start, Giovanni," Enzo muttered.

Giovanni got up from the chair, grabbed the bag of sweets and sat back down.

"Do you mind?" Shaun asked.

Throwing another into his mouth, Giovanni didn't break Shaun's icy glare once. "Not at all. I'm going to give you a lesson, Shaun. One I've been wanting to give you since we arrived here, but Enzo and Marco told me not to."

Shaun glanced at Enzo, who just shook his head. Suddenly Shaun felt nervous. Enzo and Giovanni had turned a blind eye to his frosty behaviour. He worried he had pushed them a little too far that afternoon. Giovanni held up the half-eaten bag of M&Ms. "See this?"

Shaun nodded.

"If you eat all these to yourself," Giovanni continued, helping himself to another, "you will feel sick and bloated. The enjoyment stops. But you carry on because they're yours."

Shaun just stared at Giovanni. He wasn't as handsome as Enzo. A scar on his cheek gave him an edge that screamed not to mess with him. "Go on."

"Very well, I will spell it out for you. If you share them, everyone gets enjoyment from them, and things run smoothly. No sickness, no arguments and we are a team. Are you understanding what I'm saying?"

Nodding, Shaun felt like he had been sent to the headmaster's office. That had happened more times than he cared to admit. He had been a bright student, but his mouth had always got him into trouble. It seemed things hadn't changed all that much. "I do," he said quietly. He wanted to defend his position, but he didn't dare.

Giovanni got up. "Good. I'll go and see if the others want any of these. I'll call it a peace offering from you, shall I?"

"Do what you want," Shaun said.

Giovanni lurched forward.

"Giovanni. No," Enzo shouted.

"What I want is for you to stop being a selfish little fuck." Giovanni sneered. "Marco has enough on his mind keeping us alive and stopping that oily bastard from ruining all the work we've done. You crying about not being able to have everything is starting to get seriously on my nerves."

Without waiting for a reply, Giovanni rolled an M&M into his hand and dropped it into Shaun's lap. "Enjoy," he snarled. He stormed out of the room, leaving Shaun rattled, the chocolate on his lap.

"Your good cop, bad cop routine is pretty effective," he said to Enzo.

"I really hope so, Shaun. You are making this far worse for yourself than you need to," Enzo said softly.

Shaun could see what they meant and hated himself for his stupid, childish reaction. He picked up the M&M and offered it to Enzo. "I will try. Honest I will."

Enzo took the chocolate from Shaun's palm. The contact made Shaun tingle and he stared at Enzo.

"Things could be different here," Enzo said. "So very different."

The intention in his words was unmistakable. Enzo slowly put the chocolate into his mouth.

"I'm not sure I can change the habit of a lifetime," Shaun managed.

"I think there is more to you than meets the eye, Shaun."

"Clean slate?"

Enzo nodded and once more his eyes crinkled as he smiled warmly at Shaun.

* * * *

"Hurry up, Enzo," Shaun shouted up the stairs.

Marco came out of the lounge. "You two aren't falling out on day one, are you?"

"That man spends more time in the bathroom than Dolly and Claire combined," Shaun said.

Marco laughed. He had an infectious laugh that Shaun hadn't really noticed before. "Perhaps this new arrangement will do you both good. When Uncle Z gets Wellingham under control, we'll get some builders in. One bathroom is not enough, especially if he brings a ton of men with him."

"Uncle Z is bringing a squad of hunky Italian men?" Shaun asked, perking up. "Perhaps things are on the change round here."

The bathroom door opened and Enzo's head appeared around the doorframe. "What is the bloody rush?" he shouted down the stairs.

He looked cute with his wet hair all mussed up. As he wasn't wearing a shirt, Shaun could make out muscular shoulders and a hairy chest.

"We're off to the supermarket, Enzo," Shaun replied, getting his carnal thoughts under control. "You're going to love my life. So much more exciting than drug running and protecting the girls."

Marco leant against the study doorframe. "If I didn't know any better, I'd say we're beginning to find an understanding."

Shaun hated being patronised only slightly less than he hated the taste of humble pie. "Don't push it, Marco. When Wellingham's under control, I'm out of here. Please try to remember that I don't want any part of this. If, and I say if, I make a bit more effort, it is not that I agree with any of this shit. It's for my own survival."

Holding his hands up, Marco pulled a face. "I come in peace. With that temper of yours, you could be one of my best men if we could harness it for good."

Shaun narrowed his eyes. "Good? You think what you do is good? Your business could either break my brother's heart or end his life or both."

The smile fell from Marco's face. "I would give my life for Liam. You know that."

He had no doubt that Marco truly believed what he was saying, but Shaun knew better. He might be thawing a little, but he would make sure they didn't see silence as compliance.

"He took a bullet for you, for fuck's sake," Shaun muttered. "You were conveniently off the scene when the hospital-bedside vigil was required, if I remember."

"It wasn't a good idea for me to visit. You saw that I was out of my mind," Marco replied.

The police had been sniffing around the hospital endlessly. According to Claire, as Marco had sobbed over Liam's body, she and Harry had come up with a story that a firearm had gone off by mistake. Even though they were at war, the code of organised crime was to sort it out between themselves. They would all have been arrested if the police had thought it anything more sinister.

When the blue lights and sirens had arrived at Jonny's house, they had all banded together as though they were one big happy family. Something that had made Shaun rage when he had heard.

Claire had ridden with Liam in one ambulance and Jonny with his daughter, Sadie, who he'd dragged out of the burning building, in another. But the hospital staff had known there was more to this than met the eye and kept them as far apart as possible.

Shaun hadn't seen Jonny except one time at opposite ends of a hospital corridor. He'd stopped in his tracks and just glared at Wellingham, who had glared back. Not long after, Jonny had arranged for Sadie to be transferred to a private facility in Cheadle.

"I know, but if you ever saw the consequences of your good work, you might think twice about it. It's not pretty. So, I repeat my position, this thaw is not to be seen as condoning this whole nightmare scenario. I like you, Marco, honestly I do, but if my brother wasn't with you…let's just say, I would sleep easier."

There he had said it. If Marco wanted a new open-book relationship, then that was what he would get.

"That is very honest, Shaun. I hope I can change your mind," Marco said eventually.

"I do too," Shaun replied. He meant it. If Marco could convince him of Liam's safety, then they could hopefully build something.

The conversation halted as Enzo bounded down the stairs, his large frame making each step thud. He'd thrown on a white T-shirt and black jeans. Shaun took in his body and wondered what it would feel like to be on top of him, then almost immediately banished those thoughts from his mind.

"Bloody hell, Enzo," he said. "This farmhouse is about two hundred years old but you're going to raze it to the bloody ground with your clodhopper feet."

Enzo seemed a little hurt. Shaun cursed himself. He'd meant it as a joke, but his dry wit clearly didn't translate to Italian. "Chill out," he continued. "That was a joke. You're going to have to learn a bit of humour if this is going to work."

Enzo relaxed. "I've no idea what a bloody clodhopper is anyway." He turned to Marco who shrugged.

"Me neither, truth be told," Shaun said. "Right, let's go on our mission to find supplies."

Enzo grabbed his keys from the table. "Your chariot awaits." Enzo set off towards the door.

Shaun went to follow him, but Marco held him by the arm. "I appreciate your honesty, Shaun," he said. "I want us to get along. Not just for the business. I intend on being in Liam's life for the duration. Your approval would mean a lot to me."

His face was full of sincerity. Shaun could see why Liam had fallen so hard for him.

"Let's see," he replied. "I'm not being like this to hurt either of you. I love him more than anything on this planet. I can't help but be protective. After failing to keep him away from Jonny, I need to know he will be all right with you."

Without waiting for Marco's reply, he followed Enzo out to the car.

"Are you two arguing?" Enzo asked.

The worried, furrowed brow made Shaun's heart melt. He really did seem to care.

Shaun thought about his response for a second. "I'd say we're getting to know each other."

Enzo nodded. "I suppose that is a good thing." Getting into the car, Enzo frowned at Shaun still standing there. "What?"

"I've never had a bodyguard before," Shaun said. "Do I sit in the back?"

A twinkle appeared in Enzo's eye. "I think you are mistaking a bodyguard for a chauffeur."

Shaun went round the car and got in the passenger seat. "Does that mean you don't carry all the bags and push the trolley?"

"I'm not sure if I prefer you moody or funny," Enzo said, firing the car up.

They drove down the farm track and out onto the main road. The farm sat at the top of a hill, above a small village nestled on the edge of the Yorkshire moors. Marco had chosen it because it was far enough away from the city centre that they would be hidden but still less than an hour's drive away.

Unfortunately, that meant that a supermarket was half an hour away. When Shaun had grudgingly taken on housekeeper duties, he'd found a decent one in a nearby town, but he could admit that he hadn't really made a huge effort to make the farm a happy place.

Lying awake the night before and thinking about everyone's words, he'd made a vow to change that. He might not agree with half of what this lot got up to, but he could focus on the job at hand. It would please Liam if nothing else. He had also thought about Enzo jumping in between him and Giovanni. It puzzled him why Enzo would risk an argument with his brother for Shaun. He found he quite liked the idea of someone on his team. It made him want to behave better.

They got to the shop. Enzo glanced around the car park as he locked up.

"All clear?" Shaun said half-jokingly.

"I am starting to understand that you use humour to cope with situations," Enzo said seriously. "Only, could you do me a favour?"

Intrigued, Shaun nodded. "I can try."

"Be funny."

A response formed on Shaun's lips until Enzo smiled.

"Oh, I see. It's like that, is it?" Shaun said.

"Come on." Enzo set off towards the shop. "Let's get this done."

"It's very domestic, isn't it?" Shaun said, following Enzo across the car park.

"What is?"

"This. You and me doing the weekly shop. I quite like the idea of people thinking I have an Italian hunk on my arm."

Enzo turned and raised an eyebrow. "You think I'm a hunk?"

Shaun reddened. His big mouth had given away too much. He occupied himself with getting the shopping list out of his bag. "Just get inside and stop fishing for compliments."

As he looked up, he caught Enzo staring at him. He grinned and walked into the supermarket.

It was a Thursday morning and there was hardly anyone around. Enzo seemed to relax a little bit and actually took control of the trolley. He looked completely out of his comfort zone. *Do they not have supermarkets in Italy?*

"You don't really have to push it," Shaun said.

"I think it best if you choose things, don't you?"

He had a point. They wandered farther in and were greeted by a dazzling display of Christmas decorations.

Shaun turned to Enzo. "I've had an idea."

Chapter Six

Bags spilled out on the sofa. Tinsel and shiny things were everywhere. Enzo was wide-eyed in amazement. "Do you think we got too much?" he asked.

"No such thing, babes," Shaun replied. He picked up a garland and draped it around his shoulders. "Mr DeMille, I'm ready for my close up."

Enzo frowned. "Who is Mr DeMille?"

Shaun shook his head. "I give up." He fussed with the garland along the mantlepiece.

"How long are you going to be in there?" Claire shouted through the door. "*The Chase* is on soon and Dolly will lose her shit if she misses it."

"Oh, for fuck's sake," Shaun muttered. "I try and make a bit of effort. I can't win round here, can I?"

"Chill," Enzo said, resting his hand on Shaun's shoulder. Shaun tensed. The feel of the big Italian's hand on his body making him melt. "Claire, tell Dolly to watch it in Giovanni's room. He got a new TV the other day."

There was silence for a second. Shaun tried to ignore the warmth that spread through him from Enzo lightly gripping him.

"Fine," Claire shouted. "But we like to have biscuits with it so don't blame me if he has crumbs in his bed."

Content she had been deflected, Enzo relaxed and let go of Shaun. They began rifling through the bags of things they'd smuggled into the room.

"A fancy new television, eh? Has Giovanni been splashing the cash?" Shaun asked, fiddling with a garland.

"I think we all need to make this place a bit more homely," Enzo replied. "Although I had thought about getting him one for Christmas. I'll have to think about something else now."

Satisfied with his arrangement, Shaun got some baubles out of the bag. They had pictures of Santa and his reindeers on them. "Santa Claus is comin' to town," he sang, holding them up as earrings.

Enzo burst out laughing. Shaun carried on singing and dancing around the sofa. Enzo stopped and grabbed hold of Shaun as he sauntered past. With his strong, muscular arms, he spun Shaun around until he was dizzy and they collapsed on the sofa amidst the decorations, Enzo's solid body on top of Shaun's. For a split second, Shaun thought they were going to kiss. Enzo's breath tickled his face. He wasn't sure he had the courage to clear those last few inches to find out what Enzo's lips tasted like.

But the moment was gone as quickly as it came, and Enzo scrambled to his feet.

"Hey, you've got some moves there, Enzo," Shaun said, throwing the baubles down.

"Uncle Z sent us to dance lessons as well as self-defence," Enzo explained, straightening his jumper. "He said no one knows their body like a dancer."

"Uncle Z sounds like a real card," Shaun said.

He got to his feet and wrapped another long garland of tinsel around a lamp. They hadn't got a tree. It would rather spoil the surprise if they'd dragged an eight-foot spruce pine through the house. Plus, the furniture and décor of the farmhouse had definitely seen better days. A brand-new Christmas tree with all the trimmings might be pushing things a little too far.

Shaun had tried to make things nicer in the rooms, but Marco had other things on his mind than interior design. Even so, Shaun had picked up the odd picture and cushion when he went to the supermarket and dotted them around. They had got the farmhouse with all the contents—the owner had died and his family didn't want to be bothered with it all. Marco had seen this as a good thing… Shaun wasn't so sure about that.

"What shall I do with these?" Enzo asked, holding up the two glittery baubles that Shaun had discarded.

"Ah, so many suggestions," Shaun teased. "But how about you dig around for the rest and fill that bowl with them."

He gestured to the old wooden bowl that had served as a place to keep the remote controls in.

Enzo looked impressed. "You have an eye for this, you know."

"Why thank you, sir. I love Christmas, don't you?"

Enzo absentmindedly inspected a figurine of an elf ice skating. "I guess so. I used to love it as a kid."

Shaun realised that Enzo would be spending Christmas away from his family this year. Never having had anyone other than Liam and his mother,

Shaun often forgot that other people had had better experiences in the family lotto.

Ever since he'd left Manchester, Christmas had been a time for friends. They had made a huge effort, but deep down, he'd always missed his brother. It would be fun being with him for the big day this year. He would only have eyes for Marco, but still, it would be nice to sit around a table together.

Enzo finished arranging the baubles in the bowl. "How is that?"

"Not bad," Shaun said.

But something had shifted in Enzo. He had sadness behind the seemingly forced smile. They put the rest of the decorations up in relative silence. Shaun hummed Christmas carols while they got the lights and the twinkly decorations just right.

"It's perfect," Shaun said eventually, clapping his hands together. "I think we're ready for them."

With flourish he opened the door and headed down the hall to the dining room where Liam, Giovanni and Marco were weighing out the stock and dividing it into smaller packages. Yet again Shaun found himself in another situation where even witnessing what they were doing would land him a decent stretch in prison, but he pushed it to the back of his mind. He could always try a coercion defence if it came to that.

"Don't cause a draught," Giovanni shouted.

"Oh, calm down. We need a bit of snow. It's Christmas," Marco said, winking at Liam.

"It's degrading that we're even doing this," Giovanni continued. "It wouldn't happen in Roma."

"Toto, we're not in Roma anymore. Stop being a grump. Look – even Shaun has found his smile," Marco retaliated.

Liam put his bag down and frowned at Shaun. "What's put that smile on your face, bro? Not that I'm complaining."

Shaun put on his best pout. He'd had enough of being reminded of his previous bad behaviour. *What do these people want?*

"Uh-oh, looks like it's disappeared," Marco teased. "Liam, you scared it away."

Shaun smiled and even more so when Liam, Marco and Giovanni all cheered. "Fuck off, the lot of you," Shaun replied although he had to laugh. "If you're interested in what Enzo and I have been up to, please make your way to the lounge."

Liam got up. "I need a break from this anyway. It's bloody hard work."

Marco and Giovanni also got up. Shaun led them through to the lounge. Enzo was nowhere to be found, but the others gasped when they saw it. Fairy lights lined the stone fireplace, and they had filled the mantlepiece with as many cheap figurines as possible. Baubles covered every surface and a sequinned reindeer sat in pride of place in the hearth.

"Wow, "Liam said, putting his arm around Shaun. "You've worked wonders."

"You really have," Marco said.

Giovanni just nodded. Shaun took that to be high praise indeed. He figured that Giovanni considered himself far too butch to coo over Christmas decorations.

"Where's my brother?" Giovanni asked.

"I'm here," Enzo said from the doorway. His eyes were red.

"Are you okay?" Shaun asked.

"Yeah. Managed to squirt aftershave in my eye," Enzo replied.

The look of concern that passed between Marco and Giovanni didn't escape Shaun's attention.

"Enzo, you've both done a wonderful job," Liam said, seemingly oblivious. "Thank you so much."

Enzo sat on the sofa. In his thick navy jumper and dark jeans, he resembled an Italian crooner ready to give them a song. Once more, Shaun marvelled that he'd never properly noticed the handsome man.

"It was all Shaun's idea," Enzo replied.

"Aw shucks. I can't take all the credit. You chose the reindeer," Shaun reminded him, causing him to blush.

"Bleeding hell, has a gay bomb gone off in here?" Claire said from the doorway.

"It looks amazing," Dolly added over her shoulder.

"I thought you were watching *The Chase*?" Shaun asked.

Dolly made her way in and sat next to Enzo on the sofa. "We can't work his fancy bloody television," she said, examining a snow globe of Santa mooning that Shaun had put on the table next to where Giovanni liked to sit.

"You'd better not have touched that new television," Giovanni growled. "Enzo, did you know about this?"

Dolly shook the globe. "Don't get your knackers in a knot. He gave us permission."

Giovanni huffed and stormed out of the room. His footsteps on the stairs made them all wince.

"Stroppy shite," Claire giggled. "We need a drink to officially open Shauny's grotto. One sec."

She dashed out of the room.

"What the fuck have you women done?" Giovanni shouted through the floorboards above them.

"You're in trouble now," Liam teased.

"I couldn't give a fuck," Dolly replied, replacing the snow globe. "He needs to learn to share."

There were thundering footsteps down the stairs and a red-faced Giovanni came back in the room.

"I can only find bloody Channel Five on that TV now. What did you press? You shouldn't even be in there. That is my new television and my room," he roared.

Shaun extracted himself from Liam's arm and walked over to Giovanni. "A wise man once told me, if you share things, everyone gets enjoyment from them, and things run smoothly." He turned to Enzo. "Now who was that?"

Giovanni had gone bright red. He screwed his face up. "Oh…fuck off."

Storming out of the room, he almost barged into Claire holding a tray of drinks. "Calm it. Don't threaten the booze," she shouted.

Dolly clapped her hands together as Claire put the tray down. "Ooh, fizz. Now it does feel like Christmas," she remarked, grabbing a glass.

"It's the good stuff too," Marco said. "What's the point in doing all this work if we can't have a bit of enjoyment from it?"

They all took glasses and raised them.

"To the farm," Shaun said, careful not to give the impression he had changed his disapproval of the wider issue.

"To the farm," Marco repeated with a nod to Shaun. It suggested he got exactly the intention behind his words.

They all found seats. The room was bathed in the soft, warm glow from the golden fairy lights. Shaun had wanted ones as far away as possible from the lurid technicolour strings his mother used to put up.

"If only we had a real fire," Dolly said. "When I was a lass, we'd toast crumpets on the fire on Christmas Eve. Mum would slather them in jam. They tasted so good."

Shaun had examined up the chimney with a torch, but it had been blocked up years ago. They would have to imagine it…otherwise they could burn the whole place down.

"Do you remember that year Mum got cheap balloons from the fifty-pence shop?" Shaun said to Liam. "We blew them all up and they had things on like *Carpet Sale Today* and *Happy Hanukkah."*

Liam laughed. "We put them up though."

"Course we did. Waste not want not," he replied.

Their mother had also loved Christmas. Mainly because it meant getting absolutely out of it for days on end, but to be fair to her, she would make sure they had a decent time as well. If she didn't have a boyfriend willing to part with his cash for their presents, she would go on one of her special shopping trips that involved no money changing hands but miraculously full pillowcases on Christmas morning.

"We have full-on Christmases at home," Marco said. "It will be odd to be away this year."

Shaun glanced at an uncomfortable Enzo. Shaun wondered what was bothering him. Surely it couldn't just be missing his mama at Christmas.

"But our first together," Liam said, resting his hand on Marco's thigh.

Marco sat on the arm of Liam's chair. He put an arm around his shoulder and drew him close. "Then it will be perfect," he said, beaming.

Claire sat on the rug next to the reindeer. "Christmas is ages away yet anyway. I've barely started my advent calendar."

Marco grabbed a bauble and threw it at her but missed. "Killjoy," he said with a grin.

It was nice to be in the room together, even if Giovanni had taken his sulk upstairs. It dawned on Shaun that the rest of them were used to being in that room with one person missing. But it had always been him in self-imposed exile upstairs. He hated to admit it, but it did feel good to be part of the group.

"Hey, Shaun," Claire said. "I saw an advert on that rancid-looking village hall notice board today. They're doing yoga classes. That's up your street, isn't it?"

Shaun had been missing yoga while he'd been at the farm. He would still do it every day in his room, but he loved the social atmosphere of a yoga class. They had become an obsession ever since he had travelled.

"It might not be daybreak on a beach in Goa, but I could be up for it," he replied.

Marco cleared his throat. Of course, Shaun had forgotten the restrictions currently imposed on him. But this time he wouldn't push against it. Nothing could make him spoil this moment.

"Oh, well just an idea. Thanks," Shaun said. He took a long swig of champagne to help him swallow his words down.

Enzo sat forward and placed his glass on the coffee table. "I'm still his bodyguard, no? If I go, he goes."

All eyes were on Enzo.

"You'd come to a yoga class? I thought you didn't believe in silly poses?" Shaun asked, in shock. The burly body of Enzo did not suggest it would lend itself to the contortions required for yoga.

"Pah," Enzo said, sniffing. "I'm perfectly capable of whatever they can throw at me."

Shaun glanced at Liam, who shrugged.

"Right, well, let's go stretching sometime," Shaun said, raising his glass to Enzo.

This could be fun.

Chapter Seven

The December air bit like a cranky dog as they got out of the car at the village hall. Claire hadn't been wrong when she'd said it was a bit rundown. Paint peeled from the window frames, and the curtains could have been put up during World War Two.

"What a bloody dump," Shaun grumbled. "Still, I've done yoga in worse. I went to this place in India where we had to share the room with a family of monkeys. It impacted one's ability to relax, I can tell you."

A group of women in lurid spandex eyed them suspiciously as they approached the door. Shaun had only ever driven through the village until this moment. Marco had banned them from the pub and shop. He didn't trust anyone, although Shaun seriously doubted that Jonny Wellingham's reach would stretch to this one-horse town.

"Good evening," Shaun said, with his best friendly expression. To his amazement, he actually felt nervous.

"Can we help you?" said one woman in shocking pink leggings paired with a purple bomber jacket.

"Jean, that's not very friendly," replied another resplendent in peach jogging trousers and a matching T-shirt that had *Just Do It Later* with the Nike tick across it.

Shaun glanced over at Enzo, who looked decidedly uncomfortable. Shaun found himself feeling protective over his Italian bodyguard. It had been good of him to come. They had struggled to find anything for him to wear. In the end he opted for his weightlifting jogging trousers and a vest top that showed off his muscles to full effect. Shaun had a feeling these women would change their tune once Enzo removed his jacket. They were only human, after all.

When Enzo had come down the stairs, ready to go, he had taken Shaun's breath away. Both the joggers and the vest clung to him. The temptation to abandon yoga and go and find their own positions was very strong. But that absolutely was not on Shaun's agenda, so he'd taken the mental equivalent of a cold shower and set off into the night air.

"We're here for the yoga class," he said ignoring the other interested stares. "We live up on the farm."

A few glances were exchanged. It took a strong stomach to be a newcomer in these parts. He imagined that these women had lived here all their lives. He envied the sense of belonging. He'd been a nomad most of *his* life, but after spending these weeks with Liam, he had a niggling suspicion that he wanted more. Even if the circumstances were far from ideal.

"You're very welcome," a third lady said. She was stunning, with blonde hair and an expensive-looking white parka. She had on black leggings and pumps and had a smile that could light up the whole village. At last, Shaun detected a kindred spirit.

"Thank you. I'm Shaun and this is Enzo," he replied.

The women gave Enzo approving glances.

"Does he speak?" Jean asked, peering at him.

"I do," Enzo said.

"I'm Becky," the white parka lady said.

Shaun took her hand. He clocked a very expensive manicure. Becky obviously spent a lot more on her personal grooming than the rest of her classmates.

"You enjoy yoga?" she asked.

"I love it. I spent six months touring India and got a real thing for it," he replied.

"Hark at him," Jean said. "You might be able to teach Pippa a thing or two."

A ripple of whispers passed through the others. He was just about to question them on what that meant, when suddenly a Fiat Uno that had seen better days screeched to a halt outside the hall and a woman in her mid-fifties with wild hair got out.

"Sorry, girls," she said. "Barnaby wouldn't go down. I told him Mummy had to help the ladies with their posture, but he wouldn't have it. Poor little lamb." She noticed Shaun and Enzo as though two aliens had joined her merry band. "Hello. Who have we here?"

"Hi, I'm Shaun," he said, stepping forward and holding out his hand which she took very enthusiastically. "And this is Enzo...my...uh...friend."

"And I'm so sorry to leave you standing out here. I'm Pippa. Pleased to meet you. It's not often we get newcomers to the class. I hope my ladies have been making you feel welcome."

"Shaun has studied yoga in India," Jean piped up.

Pippa regarded him in alarm. "I hope we're not a letdown for you then, Shaun."

"I'm sure it will be just fine. I've been doing it on my own for months."

"It's no fun on your own," Jean laughed, nudging the woman next to her. "Yoga, that is."

They all collapsed into fits of giggles that Shaun joined in with. He would show them he could be part of the gang, no matter what they thought.

Pippa fumbled with the keys and let them into the hall. Inside, things weren't much better than the outside. The paint job was beige and red but had so many marks and scuffs on it. They had a stage of sorts up one end. Shaun could hardly imagine what kind of productions these walls had seen.

"Everyone grab a mat from the side and make yourselves at home," Pippa barked. "It's lovely and warm. Mr Tompkinson left the heating on after indoor bowling, so no excuses."

Shaun grabbed mats for both him and Enzo and they found a spot at the back.

"You ready to flex, big boy?" Shaun whispered.

"I don't know why I volunteered to do this," Enzo muttered. He looked as though he were being led to the gallows.

Everyone hushed as Pippa cleared her throat. Shaun was ready for this now. It felt like he'd been released from prison, albeit temporarily.

"We're going to open with a sun salutation," Pippa announced.

They started working their way through the yoga poses. Nothing made Shaun more alive than his muscles tensing as he stretched and flexed. Halfway into it, he heard some grunting to his left. He peered across at poor Enzo, about two moves behind everyone else. He was struggling to hold any recognisable pose and sweat was pouring down his face.

Shaun thought about making a sly dig, but he remembered that Enzo had put himself through all this so Shaun could do something he liked. His heart melted a little as he watched him.

Enzo caught his eye and stuck out his tongue. Shaun winked and resumed his position with a warmer glow than before. Enzo might be totally unsuited to yoga, but his tight vest and rippling muscles were drawing admiring glances. Shaun could fully understand where they were coming from. As far as bodyguards went, Shaun had been given a sexy one.

An hour later and a totally revitalised Shaun couldn't wipe the grin off his face. Doing yoga online or on his own was nowhere near the same as being in a room with people. Even if they were a ragtag bunch of people who would be more at home in a Women's Institute meeting. It felt so good to be with people who didn't commit crime as casually as they went to the supermarket. He could just imagine the outrage if these women had the slightest inkling of the real story of their new neighbours up at the farm.

"Did you enjoy that?" Becky asked as he dragged his and Enzo's mats to the pile.

Poor Enzo looked as though he needed a lie down as quickly as possible. Even zipping his hoodie up seemed to be a struggle. He may be a champion weightlifter but supporting that body throughout the class had made his arms shake like jelly.

"I did. Not sure about Enzo," he replied.

"Is he your husband?" she asked.

"Oh God no," Shaun said, laughing. "Just a friend."

Becky and Shaun stopped to see Enzo hobbling over to the door. Jean was rubbing his back, which seemed to be making him turn redder.

"Most of us break wind when we first start," she said. "Don't think anything of it, love."

Shaun stifled a giggle. "Poor Enzo."

"We all go for a drink at the White Lion if you fancy it?" Becky asked. "It's a tradition."

"Why not," Shaun said. "Enzo is such a hit with Jean and her mob—it would be a shame to deprive them."

They caught up to a slow-moving Enzo and Jean, who had graduated to vigorously squeezing his biceps.

"It's just a case of getting the blood flowing again. Such big muscles. We'll have you right as rain in no time," she soothed.

Enzo looked as though he was anything but reassured.

"Becky has invited us for a drink," Shaun said.

Enzo glared at him. Shaun knew he was being evil, but he could only fight so much temptation.

"Oh, you must, Enzy," Jean said. "I want to hear all about Rome. It will help you catch your breath. Perhaps no fizzy drinks though. We don't want a repeat of what happened in the downward dog." She led Enzo out of the hall by the hand.

"He's got a fan there," Becky said.

"I'm sure he's thrilled," Shaun said, following her out of the musty-smelling hall.

They all made their way across the street to a little pub on the other side. It was pretty busy inside. It seemed the menfolk of this village took the opportunity for darts and beer while their women were making strange shapes.

Jean half dragged Enzo over to a portly man holding court by the darts board. "Stanley, up you get. This lad needs a seat. Go and get him a pint," she ordered.

Stanley leapt to attention and scuttled over to the bar. Shaun supposed that Jean never had to ask twice for anything. He couldn't really blame Stanley. Even poor Enzo had been mollified into submission under her guiding hand.

"No prizes for guessing who wears the trousers in that house," Shaun said to Becky. "Can I get you a drink?"

"A rosé for me please," she said.

"Pink wine. A woman after my own heart," he replied.

He got the drinks and, with a wink at Enzo, who had a harem of women fussing over him, he sat with Becky. He would rescue Enzo in time. "Cheers," he said, raising his own glass of rosé.

"Cheers," she replied, taking a sip. "You've kept yourselves to yourselves up there. We were beginning to think you were up to no good."

He might have known a small village would keep the farm under surveillance. He would have to be careful not to give them any cause for alarm. Footpaths led quite close to the farmhouse and Marco would go mad if he thought the villagers were watching them, no matter how innocently.

"Oh, you know how it is. Busy times," he said.

"Tell me about it. I've got a B&B in the village and I'm booked well into the new year."

Shaun frowned. It seemed strange that a tiny place like this would be a destination of choice. "Is it usually busy?"

Becky shrugged. "Never used to be, but they made that programme about a boy and his talking sheepdog in the next village. You know the one. They fight crime and run a farm. Everyone wants to come here now. Not that I'm complaining, but I was going to refurb the place over the winter."

Shaun relaxed. Marco had made him paranoid. Next, he would be suspecting Jean of being a double agent for Wellingham. At that moment her only focus was to force a post-yoga massage on Enzo, who seemed to be fighting a losing battle.

"Don't be so silly," she urged. "I was a district nurse for thirty years. You haven't got anything I haven't grappled with a thousand times before."

Jean's gang of followers were in hysterics, which made her all the more determined to get her hands on Enzo.

"I used to run a bed and breakfast in Blackpool," he said to Becky. "I know what you mean about getting the jobs done over the winter. I would give it a redecoration every year and go for something completely different."

"Sounds like you're a man in the know," Becky said.

"I wouldn't say that, but I like putting colours together," Shaun replied. Then an idea struck him. "In fact, I'm going to redo the whole farm after Christmas. It needs a spruce up."

"I'm not surprised. Old Norman didn't go in for making it nice. When he died, they cleared it out and had a sale in the hall. Most of the stuff looked like it came straight from the sixties. Hey, why don't you give me your number? Maybe we could meet sometime and discuss paint charts and wallpaper patterns?"

"You're on."

Becky handed him her phone, into which he programmed his number. Marco would probably hit the roof, but what he didn't know wouldn't hurt him.

Just as Shaun gave Becky back her phone, a shadow fell over his face and a red-faced Enzo stared down at him.

"We need to get home," Enzo said.

"I'm halfway through my drink," Shaun replied.

"Jean has gone to ask the landlord if she can give me a rub down in the store cupboard," Enzo urged. "We absolutely need to go."

As much as he didn't want this trip into normality to end, Enzo needed backup and he had done him a favour by coming.

"You'd better save him," Becky said. "Once Jean gets her claws in him, he's done for."

Enzo shuddered and glanced over at the bar where Jean had started an argument with the barman.

"This is a medical situation," she announced.

"You've been retired ten years, Jean. Leave the poor lad alone," the landlord countered.

Shaun drained his wine and got up. He placed the empty glass on the bar. "Thank you for your concern, Jean, but I'd better get him home. If he's no better tomorrow, I'll bring him down to your house."

Jean grabbed onto Enzo again, squeezing his muscular arms. The offer is always open," she said. "I'm next to the shop. Anytime."

Shaun guided Enzo out of the pub. "I think we made some friends," he said with a laugh. "Jean. definitely."

"Funny guy," Enzo replied as he staggered towards the car. "What the fuck have you done to me?"

Shaun tried his best to hide his amusement. He didn't want to humiliate Enzo too much. It had been brave of him to risk this for Shaun. "Do you need me to help you into the bath when we get home?"

Enzo stopped and turned to him. "You're a nurse now, are you?"

With his heart pumping, Shaun couldn't resist. "I can be."

The moment was charged with electricity. Shaun held Enzo's gaze until Enzo broke the moment by laughing nervously. "I can just imagine Marco's face if you told him you were my nurse. I think I'll be fine, thank you."

Shaun felt more disappointed than he should. "Oh well, the offer is there," he managed.

"I'll bear it in mind." Enzo hobbled the rest of the way to the car. "You're driving," he said with a grimace.

Shaun unlocked it and helped Enzo in. He got in his side and smiled at Enzo. "It's been a wonderful night. Thank you for doing it."

Enzo grimaced as he put his seatbelt on. "And you say this shit is good for us? I can't see it myself."

Shaun helped him with the buckle. Their hands grazed and he looked at Enzo's handsome profile illuminated in the moonlight. Shaun had the urge to lean across and kiss him.

"Remember, I'm your nurse now. If I say it's good for you, then it is."

"You know what's good for everyone, do you?"

Shaun couldn't meet Enzo's gaze. He looked down. "Everyone but me," he said. "I seem to fuck that up at every opportunity."

"You don't do so bad. When you let your guard down," Enzo replied softly. "In fact, I quite like you then."

Shaun looked up and caught Enzo's eye. He trembled as he gripped the steering wheel. "I'll keep my guard down more in future then."

"I would like that."

Unable to fight the urge any longer, Shaun leant across and kissed Enzo on the cheek.

"You got yourself a deal. Now come on. A hot bath for you. Do you need Jean to come and help you? She was a district nurse, you know."

Enzo shook his head. "Just get us out of here."

Chapter Eight

Two days after the yoga class and, much to his dismay, Shaun's body hurt in places he didn't even know he had. He hobbled down the stairs into the kitchen in full view of everyone. When he'd awoken that morning in absolute agony, he'd figured he was due a ribbing. The amusement on everyone's faces told him he hadn't been wrong.

"Uh-oh," Liam said, chuckling. "Someone's seized up."

"Sod off," Shaun huffed as he poured himself a coffee from the cafetiere.

Enzo sat at the head of the table. He looked so handsome this morning in a blue-striped shirt and jeans, his hairy chest just peeping through the top. Shaun would love to feel under there, even if his body would probably protest anything more strenuous than a bit of light exploration.

He sat down next to Enzo and blew on the coffee. "I could do with going to the shops today."

"Will we need a wheelchair?" Enzo teased.

"I wouldn't mind being pushed around by a muscle-bound Roman hunk all day," Shaun said. "If you're offering."

"I think you'd better suit a chariot," Enzo replied. "Hail Shaun, leader of us all."

Shaun bowed his head regally and took a sip from his coffee. They still had some of the Italian blend Enzo and Giovanni had brought over. God, it was good. He wondered how people who didn't have caffeine even started their day.

"I hope Uncle Z brings a case of this as well as his little army," Shaun said. "I'm getting an addiction issue."

"How long now?" Enzo asked Marco.

Marco exhaled. "He reckons he's found about twenty men. Some of the other families sent us some and let's face it, Uncle Z is a name in Rome. It didn't take long. Men are lining up to work for him."

Shaun perked up. "Sounds like we might be free soon then?"

Marco shook his head. "Uncle Z isn't happy with them. He and the boys have taken them out to the country for training. Could be a while yet."

"The boys?" Liam asked.

"More cousins," Giovanni said. "Italian families have a never-ending supply of them. But you got the best two."

He winked at Enzo, who shook his head. Change was coming and it couldn't be quick enough for Shaun. He tried to take solace in the fact that Uncle Z was thorough enough to want the best. That meant his brother would be as safe as he could be and Shaun would have his freedom. Then what? He hadn't even given it any thought.

"Looks like you're stuck pushing my trolley then, Enzo," he said eventually.

He hated to admit that he liked the idea of spending the afternoon alone with Enzo. He was a sweet man and Shaun felt he could be himself around him, a luxury he didn't take for granted these days. He was absolutely gorgeous too, which helped matters along.

"Not today," Marco said. "I need him. Our man down at the universities reckons Jonny wants to get in touch. We need to go and see him. I want both of you with me. Something feels off and I wouldn't be surprised if that piece of shit had set up an ambush."

Giovanni nodded. Enzo just shrugged to Shaun. They obeyed without question. Shaun would never get used to this life.

"Me and Doll wanted to go and check out a couple of flats for the weekend too. Can we come with you?" Claire asked.

They were still using the plan of renting apartments for a few nights in the city centre. Claire and Dolly had built up a loyal customer base who just messaged for a location if they wanted business. It kept the police off their backs, but more importantly, it meant that the likes of Jonny wouldn't know where to strike, should they wish to. The days of grotty old brothels were dying out along with Jonny Wellingham's grip on Manchester.

"Yeah, seems like a good idea," Marco said.

"Fine," Shaun said. "Can I give you a shopping list then?"

Marco got up from the table. "I don't know if we'll have time."

Shaun had no intention of begging for food. They seriously thought he would pull a gourmet meal out of thin air while they were doing whatever they were doing.

"It's up to you, boss," he declared. "If you get the stuff, we have a delicious lamb tagine for dinner. If you don't, it's fish fingers and oven chips."

"Here, give me the list," Claire said, holding out her hand. "We can sort it before we go to the flat."

Gratefully, Shaun handed her the list he'd put together in bed the night before. Running the house could be hard work sometimes. Hardly the same challenge as the bed and breakfast in Blackpool, but he found himself wanting to do a good job more and more.

Tagine was Enzo's favourite and since the great thaw, it pleased him to make Enzo happy. What did that mean?

Eventually everyone left, leaving only Shaun and Liam. For once, Shaun had nothing to do. Miraculously, they had left the kitchen in a decent state, which meant he wouldn't have to clear up after them.

"What shall we do today then, brother?" Liam asked.

Even though they had been in each other's pockets for the last three months, they rarely got time alone. Liam took his role as advisor to Marco very seriously.

"Well as we've to guard the homestead and I can't cook anything, there's only one thing for it," Shaun replied.

Liam frowned. "What's that?"

"I'm going to have to annihilate you on the PlayStation," Shaun said with a grin.

Two hours later and Shaun's eyes were going. Liam had won nearly every game. He had some kind of gaming superpowers. Shaun remembered a time when

Liam would come to him and beg him to get past a certain level. Those days were long gone.

"I surrender," Shaun cried, holding his hands up. "You're too good for me."

Liam curled up on the sofa and Shaun sat sprawled in the chair. His brother had blossomed into a handsome young man. A powerful rush of love for Liam washed over Shaun.

"It's been fun though, hasn't it?" Liam said, smiling.

"Yeah, kiddo." Shaun returned the grin. "It's nice to have a bit of time with you. Just you and me."

Liam carefully replaced the two controllers. Marco had bought him the console soon after he'd come out of hospital to replace the one he'd lost when Wellingham's gang turned Liam's flat over.

He'd always been a video game addict, ever since one of their mother's boyfriends had acquired a second-hand one from somewhere. Shaun supposed it had been a form of escape. He envied him that. Being the older of the two, he had always been front and centre of whatever current drama played out in their mother's life.

It was sweet the way Liam treasured the console though. It meant so much to him that Shaun made a mental note to speak to Marco about his Christmas present plans for Liam. Shaun guessed that he wouldn't have had time to sort anything all that special. Knowing his brother like he did, that would be devastating to him. Shaun would see if he could help. It would be a bonding exercise for them. God knew, they needed it.

"You really love him, don't you?" Shaun said.

Surprised at the direct question, Liam curled up on the couch and a vomit-inducing misty expression appeared on his face. Once again Shaun marvelled that his kid brother was all grown up.

"I think I do," Liam said eventually. "I've never been in love before, so I don't know, really."

"I bloody do. Look at you." Shaun laughed. "Sickly smile? Check. Primal noises coming from the bedroom? Check. Risking your life for his? Check. Yeah, you got it bad, bro."

Liam smiled shyly. "Don't take the piss."

Shaun instantly regretted his acidic tongue. His brother had found happiness, and even though they were still in a shit ton of trouble, Shaun was genuinely pleased. He might have serious reservations about Marco's choice of work, but he couldn't deny their love. Neither could leave the other one alone if they were in the same room. They were always stealing glances or holding hands when they thought no one was looking.

"Sorry, you know me. I couldn't be soppy if my life depended on it," Shaun said hurriedly.

He'd never been one for public displays of affection. When he'd been with Billy, they'd had a strict understanding that all the touchy-feely stuff was for the bedroom alone. It probably came from years of having to suffer his mother mauling one man or another. As a teenager, that had been beyond mortifying.

"It's me who should be sorry," Liam said. "Dragging you into this. It won't be forever, then you can head back to Blackpool and pretend like nothing happened."

Shaun stretched then winced. His legs were screaming in agony. *Fucking yoga.*

"I'm not sure I will," he announced. "Go back to Blackpool, I mean."

Liam sat up, intrigued. "You won't? I thought you couldn't wait to get there."

"Nah. It's a shithole. If anything, the last few months have taught me I want to find a bit more adventure in life," Shaun replied. "Not one that will get me killed, preferably, but I've got stuck in a rut. Time to get out of it, I think."

He'd spent a lot of time thinking in his room. When he'd left Manchester, he had been dead set on having a wild time. At first, travelling the world and seeing all the iconic sights had been everything to him. But then he'd met Billy and they'd spent time in India. That was when the yoga bug had hit. Billy had lived in Blackpool all his life and one night, while watching the sun go down, they'd had the bright idea of opening a yoga bed and breakfast near the seafront.

Their relationship hadn't lasted the course, but the guest house had proven popular. They were rarely empty. He and Billy had been better suited to being friends and Shaun had found that he quite enjoyed playing the host.

"Is Billy still calling?" Liam asked.

Shaun looked away, unable to meet his gaze. "Not for a bit. I had to be cruel to be kind. I'll make it up to him one day."

"Do you still have feelings for him?" Liam ventured.

"Fuck no," Shaun said. "That ship sailed a long time ago. But I liked working with him. I'll miss it. But this whole nightmare has made me realise life is precious. All we have to do is survive this, then your beloved can bankroll me a trip. I think it's the least he can do."

"Marco won't let you get hurt," Liam said quietly.

A hint of annoyance fluttered in Shaun. Liam seemed to think that Marco was fully in control of things. Shaun didn't have the same faith in the young man. He had been great when Shaun had been running for his life at the markets, but he'd still been in grave danger. Danger that Marco had put him in. However, they were having a lovely afternoon together and he didn't want to spoil it by reverting to his sulky self. "Well, that's reassuring," he managed.

"What will you do then?" Liam asked quickly. He seemed as keen to change the subject as Shaun. "If you're not going back to Blackpool?"

Shaun's plans weren't final by any means, but he'd had a brainwave since braving Pippa's yoga torture. "Despite the fact my body is telling me otherwise, I really enjoyed the class the other night. I think I fancy opening a retreat somewhere abroad. A brand-new start to forget all this shit."

Liam pondered that for a second. "I think that's a really good idea. Once this uncle and his mob turn up, we still don't know how long it will take to finish Jonny. I'll speak to Marco. I'm sure he can help you financially. It's the least we can do."

He hadn't considered where he would go. The problem with choice was that it all sounded good until the time came to make it into a reality. That was when things got complicated. But the prospect that Marco could hold the keys to his dreams gave Shaun a brand-new perspective on things.

"Really?" he said, perking up. "That would be great. I might start making some plans then."

"Sounds good."

"But before that, I need a hot bath. These muscles need to sort themselves out if I'm going to even think about making dinner later."

* * * *

"Hurry up and get out of there. I'm dying for a piss."

Shaun ignored him.

"Shaun, I'm not joking."

The fact they only had one bathroom for seven people was ridiculous. He'd been in there about half an hour and the boiling hot water gave his muscles life. He had absolutely no intention of moving. Another loud series of bangs on the door sent him into a rage.

"Giovanni, will you just piss outside?" Shaun shouted. "I'm having a moment to myself. Jesus Christ."

"It's December. It's bloody freezing."

But it went quiet. He let his body relax again. Grumpy Giovanni couldn't be more different from Enzo. Shaun's body tingled when he thought about the gentle giant. He was fully aware that Enzo had done and would continue to do bad things, but when they were together, it felt like all that belonged to someone else.

But Enzo had a sadness to him and Shaun had no clue what that could be. He had definitely been crying in the bathroom the day they had put the decorations up. Shaun didn't like to ask anyone. He didn't suppose Enzo would appreciate him snooping into his business. If he wanted to tell him, he would.

Even though Shaun bitterly resented losing his freedom like this, he had missed being with his bodyguard that day. However, it had been so nice to be with Liam. His brother had matured into a decent guy. He wondered if he had Harry or Jonny to thank for that.

All of a sudden, the door burst open. The bathwater slopped over the edge as Shaun struggled to hide his bits from a furious Giovanni.

"Fucking hell, you absolute nutter," Shaun shouted. "You've broken the bloody lock."

Giovanni went over to the toilet and proceeded to take a leak. "I don't give a shit. I'm not pissing in a farmyard for anyone."

Shaun instantly got out of the bath and pulled a towel around him.

"You are bang out of order. I'm not having this."

With that, he stormed out of the bathroom. Every time he seemed to make progress, one of these idiots would set him back.

Marco would be hearing from him and immediately.

Chapter Nine

Shaun slammed the baking tray of fish fingers down on the kitchen worktop. It was closely followed by one filled with oven chips. They spilled out onto the surface.

Marco, Enzo, Liam, Giovanni, Claire and Dolly all sat at the table. They had forgotten the shopping and Marco had refused to listen to Shaun when he had come downstairs to complain about Giovanni. Two things that had plunged his mood from optimistic to downright livid.

Feeling like one of the dinner ladies at school who had slopped out the revolting culinary creations to him as a kid, Shaun divided the reheated food across the plates. He placed two in front of Marco and Liam. They had the good grace not to make any comment.

"Dinner is served. Sorry it's so beige but I'm not a bloody miracle worker," he muttered. He went to the countertop and took another two, giving them to Claire and Dolly.

"Aren't there any baked beans at least?" Claire asked.

Shaun reared up. He had absolutely no intention of taking feedback on this shitty meal. "Yes, I believe they're in the aisle with the other canned foods, Claire," he sniped. "In the fucking supermarket." He picked up two more plates and gave one to Enzo before sitting down with the other.

"What about mine?" Giovanni asked.

"You can get it yourself," he muttered. "You're lucky I've even made you some."

The food on his plate made his stomach turn. Truth be told, he did have some mince and frozen vegetables in the freezer, but if no one could be bothered to go to the shop for him, he wouldn't be making them anything more exciting than this.

Giovanni seemed about to retaliate, but Marco shook his head. *A small mercy from Marco at least.* Giovanni huffed and grabbed his plate, slamming it down on the table.

They ate in silence.

"Hey, Shaun," Giovanni said when he'd finished his meagre portion. "Did you know that supermarkets deliver these days?"

Shaun raised his eyebrows. "Marco and I discussed this. He doesn't want strangers wandering around the farm. I thought you would have realised that, being an old hand at this."

Liam glanced nervously at the others. Marco finished his meal. "Well, that was very nice, Shaun. Thank you and I'm sorry we fucked up. It's been a bit of a day. You are right to be annoyed. I promise it won't happen again."

The worry etched on the young man's face made Shaun feel bad for being cranky. He expected he would get another lecture from Dolly at some point, but a man's bath should be sacred, not include Giovanni pissing inches away from his head.

"Talk to us," Liam soothed, rubbing Marco's arm. "What's happened?"

"That bastard has been putting the hard word on some of the venues," Marco said. "He's got no stock but he's threatening to torch their places if they deal for me. He's going to start a bloody drought."

Marco looked tired. For the umpteenth time, Shaun wondered when this uncle would make an entrance to ease the burden from them all. *Talk about dragging it out.*

"What are you going to do?" Liam asked.

"I'm going to put out a message that anyone caught working for Jonny Wellingham will get a lifetime ban from our business," Marco replied. "No dealers. No girls. Nothing. We have the supply lines, and we have the muscle coming. Jonny is grasping at straws."

The table fell silent. It seemed like a bold move based on goodwill. This power struggle seemed to have no end in sight. Shaun could sense Marco's weariness and understood exactly where he was coming from.

"You need to remember that Wellingham had this town sewn up for years," Dolly said. "You're asking people to take a leap of faith on you. They don't know you, love."

Marco smiled, reaching across to take her hand. "But they know you and my beloved here."

Dolly squeezed his hand. "You're a clever fucker. What do you want us to do?"

He sat in his chair, grinning at the table. Shaun could well understand why Liam had fallen hook, line and sinker for this exceptionally handsome young man.

"You, Giovanni and my Liam are going out for a drink in town," Marco said. "You can spread the word that the streets are ours and woe betide anyone who gets in our way."

"What about me, boss?" Enzo asked.

"I need you to go to the lock-up. Make sure no one is following you," Marco said. "Once they've told the dealers what's what, they'll need stock. We can get it to them tomorrow."

Enzo nodded. A wave of jealousy washed over Shaun. Once again, he would be left alone. But it wasn't just that. He missed spending time with Enzo.

"A long night beckons for me then. Shall I clean the cooker or vacuum the landing? The choice is overwhelming," he muttered.

They all jumped as Marco slammed the table with his hand, making the plates and glasses jangle.

"Honestly? I don't give a fuck what you do," Marco shouted. "Every time I'm trying to think about what to do next, you're bitching."

Shaun had only half been joking, but he wasn't prepared to make a humiliating climb-down in front of the others. Especially Giovanni. But Enzo stood before he had a chance to open his mouth.

"I think you're being unfair, Marco," he said, his voice booming through the kitchen.

Marco seemed taken aback that Enzo would turn on him like this, but soon regained his composure. If anyone had been raised to lead, it was Marco Ponti.

"Is that right?" he sneered. "My humblest of apologies, Shaun. If you could clean the cooker, it would be most appreciated. Thank you so very much."

Shaun had a hundred snarky responses, but instead he nodded and got up from the table. He smiled at Enzo to thank him for defending him. So much for trying to toe the line. He would come downstairs with the best intentions in the world, then the little devil on his shoulder would force him to be a catty bitch, willing to wind everybody up.

Instead of getting stuck into the cooker, he went through to the lounge. He had no intention of being a modern-day Cinderella for anyone. Still pouting, he switched on the television and ignored the goodbyes that came his way as the others left the house. Everyone had a mission but him. This limbo land was driving him slowly crazy.

Silence descended except for the programme he wasn't really watching, blaring out how to make a wartime dress using bits of old fabric. He jumped when Marco appeared in the doorway.

"I thought you would have gone to supervise the others," Shaun said quietly.

Marco sat on the sofa. "I'm surplus to requirements."

"I know the feeling," Shaun countered.

They sat in silence for a minute or two, both focusing on a show they had no interest in. Shaun knew that Liam would have gone to town worried about him and Marco being alone in the farm. He decided he would try again, if for no other reason than he wanted to please Liam.

"Have you thought about what you're getting our Liam for Christmas?" he ventured.

Marco sighed. "I know one thing he would like more than anything, but I think it's an impossible mission."

Intrigued, Shaun turned to him. "What's that?"

"He wants you and me to get on."

"I'll do you a deal," Shaun replied. Marco raised an eyebrow. "If I put a muzzle on my big gob, will you please consider giving me a bit more freedom? It's been a week since what happened in town and nothing. Jonny had a go, but he won't give a fuck about me, not really."

"What are you thinking?"

"Let me just go to yoga on my own. I don't think Enzo could cope with another session. Even if the ladies love him."

Marco stared at him. "You like Enzo, don't you?"

"He's okay," Shaun said, his face heating. "He's better than his gobshite brother."

"Is that part of you muzzling your mouth?" Marco asked with a smirk.

Shaun realised he had failed at the first hurdle. This would be harder than he'd reckoned. "Whoops. Sorry."

"It's fine. Giovanni is a gobshite but he's dedicated. He loves his brother more than anything as well."

"He's not all bad then."

"But I think your feelings for Enzo are deeper than you're letting on," Marco continued.

Marco's directness took some getting used to. Shaun respected him for that, but he also didn't like being under the glare of Marco's spotlight. "This is hardly an atmosphere to start a relationship, even if I wanted to," he managed.

Marco fiddled with the remote control. "If I tell you something, will you promise to keep it a secret? No one knows about this. Not Giovanni and not Liam."

"Of course. I may have a big mouth, but I can keep it shut. I'm determined to prove that to you."

Marco's face relaxed at the thaw in Shaun. "Okay, I will trust you. There was a man in Naples. Carmine," Marco said. "He came from a village outside the city and worked for us down there for many years. Enzo and he... Well I wouldn't say they were in love, but they were definitely lovers."

The pang of jealousy surprised even him. "You're talking past tense," he said.

Marco looked as though the weight of the world were on his shoulders. "I am. He was killed when the police ambushed us in Napoli."

Shaun remembered when they were putting the Christmas decorations up. Enzo must have been thinking of this Carmine...perhaps plans they had made.

"Why the cloak and dagger?" he asked. "Giovanni knows Enzo's gay, doesn't he?"

Marco nodded. "Carmine had a wife. Yes, I know it's not perfect, but it happened and it's not for me to judge. One of the reasons I asked Uncle Z to send Enzo and Giovanni was to give him something new to focus on."

In a second, he could understand why Liam had fallen for Marco. His genuine concern for Enzo endeared him to Shaun. He didn't see his cousins as pawns to move around in this never-ending game of chess. He might be intent on taking Jonny down, but Shaun saw a glint of what life could be like once that mission had been achieved. Marco would be fair.

"I will be careful," he said quietly. "I promise I will. Let's get through this, then we'll see."

Marco shifted on the sofa. "Liam tells me you want to open a yoga retreat somewhere."

Shaun nodded.

"I think we can help out with that. Leave it with me," Marco continued.

It felt as though he was being rewarded for being a good boy, but Shaun wasn't above taking a helping hand when needed. "Thank you. I mean that," he said. "I've got a small piece of advice for you though."

Marco looked intrigued. "Go on."

"If you think that's enough for Liam to unwrap on Christmas morning, you've got another think coming," he said with a grin. "I suggest you choose some things online and let me and laughing boy go and get them for you. It will save endless moaning on the day."

Marco nodded. "Received loud and clear. I'll go get my laptop and you can give me some advice."

After Marco slipped out, Shaun was rooting under the table for his notebook and pen when his phone vibrated. On checking, he saw a text message from Becky in the village.

Hi Shaun, I hope you're well. I'm sitting here with paint charts and pink wine. I wondered if you fancied giving me a hand with both?

He'd really enjoyed talking to Becky. Marco would forbid him from going, but Shaun truly believed Wellingham had gone back to ground. It was hardly likely that he would be waiting at the gates for Shaun to leave. They were all so paranoid.

Give me half an hour.

Marco came back into the room.

"Listen, Marco, I think I'm going to hit the hay," Shaun said, stretching. "My legs are still sore and I need to lie flat. You make a list and I'll sort it for you."

A little crestfallen, Marco nodded. "Oh, okay. Well, thank you, Shaun. I really think we've turned a corner tonight."

Shaun smiled. "Yes, only good times ahead. Yeah?"

Chapter Ten

He left the television on in his bedroom and stole down the landing. He took extra care to avoid the creaky floorboard that Giovanni seemed to insist on standing on every time he walked up and down...usually when Shaun had just drifted off to sleep.

Marco had the senses of a bat, so Shaun didn't dare try to creep downstairs. However, Dolly's room overlooked the lean-to where they kept the wood and coal. He could easily climb out of the window and shuffle his way to the ground.

Sneaking in, he ignored the overpowering scent of perfume. Did she bathe in the stuff? Gently, Shaun opened the window and climbed out. The cold wind hit him like a sledgehammer. *Is this really worth it?*

After the ceasefire he and Marco had called that night, he would probably regret this. But when Shaun wanted to do something, it would eat away at him until he did it. Getting the message from Becky had made him feel normal. Being invited to a friend's house for a glass of wine was something he had taken for granted before all this. Now he even considered going round a supermarket on his own a luxury.

He edged his way down the rickety roof, praying it would hold his weight. He would look like a prize idiot if he crashed through and had to explain himself. His trainers scrunched on the cold gravel as he hit the ground. Glancing around, he couldn't see anyone. The moon was high in the sky. Dusting himself off, he made his way towards the village.

Shaun didn't fancy wandering down the long and windy farm track on his own at night. Liam had found a shortcut through the woods not long after he'd come home from hospital. He and Shaun had done a proper sweep of the farm to find out possible weaknesses. To be fair, Marco had already done it, but he was happy to let Liam feel involved.

He scurried into the woods. The darkness enveloped him, but it would only take ten minutes maximum. He set off down the path.

Halfway in and Shaun had doubts whether he'd made a sensible decision. The darkness was playing tricks on him, making him feel that people were following his steps. He reached for his mobile phone in his pocket for reassurance. He hated the bloody countryside. He'd always been more of a townie.

Lights from the houses on the edge of the village started to show and he breathed a sigh of relief. Laughing to himself, he thought how silly he'd been, allowing himself to be spooked.

Suddenly a stick cracked, and Shaun whirled around. He could have sworn he saw something move, but when he shone the torch, he couldn't see anything.

His pulse was beating in his ears like the soundtrack to an Ibiza club.

"Who's there?" he shouted, amazed at how brave he sounded when in reality he was terrified.

He always wondered why people did that in films. Did many assailants reply with a "Okay you got me"? But now it seemed like the natural thing to do. Like asserting his dominance over the situation.

Either way, silence reigned. He felt stupid for even worrying. "It could have been a deer, you daft bastard," he muttered to himself.

He resumed his journey although this time he went markedly faster and could have cried with joy when he climbed the stile out of the wood. He found himself in the car park for the village hall. *There's something reassuring about tarmac when you've been dashing through a dark wood pursued by imaginary beasts.*

Becky lived at the other edge of the village. Shaun got there in record time. As usual, the place was like a ghost town. He only encountered a couple on their way to the pub. There wasn't much else to do round here.

The Nook Bed and Breakfast had originally been the vicarage and lay up a drive, overlooking the churchyard…which did nothing for Shaun's twitchiness. He took in the cosy lamps lighting the windows. He would be quite content staying here for a cheeky weekend away. *Chance would be a fine thing.*

He'd picked one of the coldest nights he could remember to go walkabout, so he didn't linger long before knocking on the door. Becky flung it open, holding a glass of rosé wine which she handed to him.

"Do come in," she said, ushering him through the door.

He took the glass and stepped inside. "Now that is a greeting."

Following Becky into the house, he examined his surroundings. The décor made him feel instantly at home. She had chosen muted tones of dusky pink, grey and pops of mustard. He had no idea why she would want to change it.

Becky took his coat and steered him into the lounge. The colour scheme continued in here, with a teal sofa sitting in the centre and a mismatch of vintage armchairs.

"It's gorgeous," he exclaimed.

"Oh, I'm bored of it now," she said, sinking down on the sofa and patting the space next to her. "One of my male guests said he felt as though he'd woken up in the pages of *Tatler* or something. I think I need to make it a wee bit more unisex."

Shaun could understand that, but it seemed a pity. Everything in here screamed expensive. Becky didn't seem to be the type to cut corners.

"What have you got in mind?" he asked, taking a slug of the wine.

"That's where you come in," she said. "I haven't invited you here just for your dazzling wit and good looks, you know."

"Well, that's a first. My good looks usually suffice," Shaun replied.

"Poor baby. It comes to us all," Becky replied.

Shaun frowned. "What does?"

"Old age." She burst into laughter. "Your face."

She might have been joking but Shaun felt slightly perturbed. He wasn't that old, for God's sake.

"I'll let that slide seeing as this wine is top drawer," Shaun said, taking a long gulp. "Come on then, show me everything."

She gave him a grand tour of the property. There were six good-sized bedrooms and a residents' television room where she served breakfast in the morning. That left a bedroom, kitchen and the lounge for herself. She had a cosy set-up and it made Shaun miss Blackpool. He might have no intention of returning, but he would absolutely find a life with the same level of simplicity and freedom after this nightmare.

"When my husband left, I had no idea what to do. I didn't fancy rattling around here turning into a mad old woman with cats," she explained. "The TV show was a blessing. It's really put this place on the map."

"How long ago was that?" Shaun asked.

She poured the remainder of the first bottle of wine into their glasses. "Hold that thought," she said, and in seconds, she'd brought a second bottle.

"You don't mess around," Shaun said, already a little tipsy.

"No point in half measures." Becky sat again.

"I can't be too late though," Shaun said, taking another big gulp of wine.

"Do you turn into a pumpkin?" she teased.

"Put it this way—you don't want to meet my ugly sisters." He needed to get there before the others. It would be impossible to sneak into the farm if it were full. It was just past nine now. He would give it another half an hour.

"So come on," Shaun continued. He didn't want to ruin the moment. "You were going to tell me all about your husband."

"Ugh. Go on then..."

But a loud knock at the door stopped her in her tracks. She frowned.

"That's odd. I don't have any guests in tonight. Who is it at this time?"

As she started to get up to answer the door, an uneasy feeling gripped Shaun. "Wait."

"What?" she asked then froze at the sound of fear in his voice.

Another loud knock rang through the house. The way the person was banging made Shaun's skin crawl. It did not sound friendly. "You're not expecting anyone?" he whispered.

"Not at this time, no," she replied. "Jean probably saw you heading up the drive. She'll be sniffing round to see if Enzo is with you. I'll get rid of her."

Unease had given way to panic. "Is there a way to see who it is?"

Becky frowned. "Are you on the run or something?"

Another loud knock. They weren't giving up. Becky got up to answer it, but Shaun beat her to the door, barring her way.

"I mean it, Becky," he urged. "We need to see them before you open that door."

"You're scaring me, Shaun," Becky said, worry etched on her face. "Is this a wind-up?"

"I wish it was." Shaun shook his head. "I'm sorry, but you're going to have to trust me on this one. Please let me see who it is before you answer it. I'm begging you. For both our sakes."

A serious Becky nodded, and they crept through to the television room. It had a bay window next to the porch. His heart racing, Shaun made his way into the room.

"You sure you saw him go in here?" said one gruff male voice from outside. So much for Jean on the hunt for Enzo.

"Absolutely," came another. "You said to ring you if I saw any of them in the village. I took the dog out and saw him coming through the woods, so I followed him. Where's my gear? You said you had good stuff."

Becky joined Shaun. "That's Frank, Jean's grandson," she whispered. "He promised her he'd stopped taking drugs. Who are these people?"

Fear ran up the back of Shaun's neck. This had been a stupid idea. He could see it now. His body was paralysed with indecision. Would they give up that easily?

"I'm ringing the police," Becky said.

"No. You can't."

"I can do what I like in my own home, thank you."

All he'd wanted was a drink and a bit of real life for an hour or two, but it had got out of control. Shaun knew what to do. He got his phone out and dialled.

"Shaun?"

"Enzo. I'm in the shit," he whispered. "I came to Becky from yoga's house for a drink and now there's someone hammering on the door."

"How many?" Enzo asked without missing a beat. Did nothing rattle this man?

Shaun peered around the curtain again. He could see two men and a younger one who must be Frank.

"Two and a villager," he replied. He wasn't even trying to keep the fear out of his voice now.

"Get upstairs and barricade yourselves in somewhere. I'm on my way home—about ten minutes away, but I'll make it five."

The call terminated. To Shaun's horror, Becky was also dialling on her mobile. He swatted it out of her hand, and it fell onto the laminate flooring.

"What—"

But he put his hand over her mouth. "I'm so sorry. I shouldn't have come here tonight. I've put you in danger, but believe me, if you get the police down here, we're fucked."

"Did you hear something?" one of the men outside said.

A figure appeared at the window and peered in. Shaun locked eyes with the man and for a second his world became tunnel-visioned. He didn't recognise the figure staring back at him but the cruel smile on his face could belong to any bad bastard in Manchester.

"Evening," the man said.

Shaun dragged Becky out of the room.

"Which is the best room to protect ourselves?" he urged. "Think quickly."

"My bedroom," she stammered. "I've got pine furniture. We can use it to block the door."

"Show me."

Becky led him up the stairs, along the landing. They made it into a room with a huge bed, armchair and mismatched vintage furniture.

"What the fuck is going on, Shaun?" Becky demanded, slamming the door behind them.

Shaun dragged a chest of drawers towards the door. "Help me," he panted.

To her credit, Becky did as he asked, and they pulled the furniture so it blocked the entrance.

"I want you to answer me," Becky snapped.

Shaun couldn't lie to her. Not now. "My fucking brother decided to fall in love with a gangster and dragged me into it."

Becky sank down on the end of the bed. "And now you've done the same for me. What the fuck, Shaun?"

He hadn't meant to put anyone in danger. Tears filled his eyes. He was so tired of this bullshit situation. "I didn't mean to."

"But you have," she said.

Shaun nodded miserably.

"Who did you call?"

"A friend," Shaun said. "He'll know what to do. He said for us to wait it out in here. He's nearly home."

A huge crash reverberated throughout the house. It was the unmistakable sound of a door being kicked in.

"They're in the fucking house!" Becky screamed. "Ring the police."

"I can't," Shaun replied. "If I do that, fuck knows where it will end."

"I don't care about your criminal code of conduct. There are intruders in my home!"

"Shh," Shaun begged. He sat down next to her on the bed and put his arm around her. She had every right to be absolutely furious with him, but she did allow him to give what little comfort he could offer.

If they spent their time arguing, the noise would direct the men to the room. The best hope they had would be them to waste time checking each one and giving Enzo the chance to get there.

"Who are these people?" Becky whispered.

But before Shaun could answer, the blade of an axe smashed through the door panel. Shards of wood flew everywhere.

This time both Becky and Shaun let out blood-curdling screams.

Chapter Eleven

They huddled together on Becky's bed. Her whole body was rigid with fear and Shaun's wasn't much better. Why on earth had he got them into this?

With the second axe blow, wood splintered everywhere, falling onto the chest of drawers. Becky screamed again at the top of her voice.

"You have to let me ring someone," she shouted, scrambling around for her mobile phone. "They're going to fucking kill us."

Shaun took the phone out of her hands. If the police got involved, they'd be all over the farm in minutes. There was enough incriminating evidence there to put all of them away for a long time. He couldn't let her do that.

"Get over by the window," Shaun ordered. "If they do get in, it's me they want. You'll have to jump for it."

"I can't jump. I'll break my fucking legs," Becky wailed.

Even so, she dashed over to the window. Cowering, she stared at him, her eyes pleading for him to do something. To take this away from the perfect little home she had created and shared with others.

It was going to be up to him to defend them. Shaun scanned the room for something to use as a weapon. *Where the fuck is Enzo?*

It all seemed horribly familiar, the adrenaline coursing through his body and the fact that two terrifying men were after his hide. But this time he'd got someone totally innocent caught up in the crossfire. He would not let Becky suffer for his stupidity. Instead of running like he had in Manchester, he had every intention of fighting.

Once again, the axe slammed against the door, knocking the panel clean out. A face appeared in the hole like a gruesome recreation of *The Shining*. He could be younger than Shaun and had on a black hoodie. He didn't look all that well built though—Shaun thought he could probably take him if he had to.

"You're fucked now," the young lad sneered, clearly feeling the same way about Shaun.

With bravery he never knew he had, Shaun ran across the room. On the way he grabbed a vase from the windowsill and smashed it over the head that was exposed. The lad staggered back, blood forming on his forehead. He looked dazed but still fully conscious. Shaun had half expected to knock him out, but he supposed that only happened in the movies.

"Fuck off," Shaun screamed through the hole in the door. He knew how ridiculous he must sound but he couldn't think of anything else. He just wanted everything to stop. He should have phoned Marco instead of Enzo. Marco would have been here by now. But Shaun had been way too concerned with covering himself.

The lad wiped the blood from his face. "You're going to pay for that, you piece of shit," he shouted.

But Shaun wasn't about to give up that easily. Once more he scanned the room for potential weapons. This time he took hold of a nail file from the bedside table. The lad tried to push the drawers away from the outside, so Shaun stabbed his hand with the file. It wasn't solid enough to go in and splintered, but it did enough damage to make the lad pull his hand back.

"Aleck, get the fuck up here," the man shouted.

"Someone's trying to get in," came the response. "You get down here."

Please God let this be Enzo.

The man glared at Shaun and disappeared down the hallway. He turned to Becky, who seemed paralysed with fear. She leapt out of her skin when a huge crash reverberated around the landing. Shaun saw the lad come flying backwards.

"Get out of my fucking way," Enzo's voice boomed.

"He's here," he said more to himself than Becky.

It didn't take long for the lad to right himself and he flung himself back down the landing. Shaun could hear Enzo cry out. Even though he was terrified, Shaun couldn't just sit there while Enzo took on the two men single-handedly. Shaun had got them into this, and he would do his best to get them out of it.

"Come on." He gestured to Becky who was still over by the window.

He heaved at the drawers but he could barely move them.

"Fucking finish him," one of the lads screamed.

Shaun had no idea what weapons they had. Every fibre of his being needed to get out to Enzo.

"What the fuck are you doing?" Becky shouted. "Don't move that!"

"He needs our help," Shaun argued. "We can't just leave him out there!"

Becky remained rooted to the spot. Shaun found strength he didn't know he had and with an almighty groan, he managed to move the drawers. The door opened a crack and Shaun slid his body through it. Maybe Becky shouldn't see anything more of this. God knew what would happen to her after this, but the less she could tell the police, the better.

On the landing, Shaun made it just in time to see one of the men land a punch squarely on Enzo's jaw, making him stagger for a second. The other man appeared at the top of the stairs. He looked dazed but to Shaun's horror, he had hold of a garrotte. The man wrapped it around Enzo's throat and pulled. Enzo's eyes immediately began to bulge and he grasped at the wire that dug deep into his flesh, blood instantly oozing over his desperate fingers.

Shaun launched himself at the attacker. Knowing his slighter frame wouldn't be enough to overpower him, he resorted to old-fashioned fighting, reaching for the assailant's face and digging his nails into him. It might not be bare-knuckle fighting, but his sole aim was to get the man off Enzo.

"Fuck you," the man grunted, trying to shake him, but Shaun wouldn't let go. The second intruder pulled at Shaun's shirt, but Shaun had a firm grip. He dug his fingers into the assailant's eyes, making him scream. With all his power, Shaun shoved the man's head backwards, causing him to loosen his grip. Enzo struggled free and leant against the wall, gasping for air.

No matter how determined he was, Shaun couldn't fight two of them. He could only focus on one, so he turned to the man he'd smashed with the vase. Shaun went to punch him but he dodged and gave Shaun a backhander that sent him falling to the floor. He cracked his head against the wall as he fell, and for a second disorientation overwhelmed him, but he scrambled to his feet as his jaw throbbed and he saw stars.

Both men had recovered enough to make another attack. Shaun had no intention of that garrotte making contact with either him or Enzo again and prepared to defend himself.

Enzo seemed to have recovered enough and he grabbed the man nearest to him, slapping him hard around the head. The other one launched himself at Shaun, but he was ready this time. He grabbed the lad's hair and yanked his head back, stopping him in his tracks.

"Fucking bastard," the lad yelled.

Shaun tugged harder.

"Run," the other shouted as he wriggled out of Enzo's clutches and shoved him hard, making him trip backwards and collapse against the wall. The man Shaun had in his grip kicked him hard in the ankle, causing him to lose his footing. He fell to the floor with a thud.

"You haven't heard the last of this, Italian scum," one of the men spat and placed a hard kick in Shaun's chest, causing him to cry out. Without waiting for Round Three, the two men ran down the stairs.

To Shaun's relief, they appeared to be leaving the house, slamming the door in the process. Enzo rubbed his neck where a fiery red line had appeared.

Shaun got to his feet and ran over. "Oh my God, Enzo. Are you all right?"

Enzo seemed dazed but fine. Suddenly he grabbed Shaun, pulling him close. Their lips met, and this time Shaun's legs buckled under him for a completely different reason. With the adrenaline still coursing around his system, he returned the kiss with a ferocity he didn't know he had. As if knowing the effect the kiss would have on him, Enzo placed his hand in the small of Shaun's back to steady him.

He had been thinking about what it would be like to kiss Enzo ever since they'd had that thaw on the moors the week before—and it was better than he could have dreamt. The smell of Enzo's woody cologne and the feel of his stubble grazing Shaun's skin set his nerves on fire. Shaun never wanted to let go of Enzo. Once more he was a touchstone for Shaun to overcome abject terror.

"Is someone going to tell me what the fuck just happened?" Becky stood on the landing, with a face like thunder. "And why my house is in tatters?"

They sprang apart like two guilty teenagers. Shaun could hardly look at Enzo. Shaun went over to her. "Becky. Oh my God, I am so sorry. I don't know what to say."

Shaking with what Shaun guessed was either fear or rage or both, Becky just glared at them. He reached out, but she sprang away, slapping his hand, her eyes wild.

"Who the hell are you?" she shouted. "Either of you?"

"You don't need to know that," Enzo replied, stepping forward between Becky and Shaun. "It's best not to. Believe me. If anyone asks, you and Shaun got drunk and tried to rearrange the place. That is your story and you stick to it. Do you understand me?"

"This is gang stuff, isn't it?" Becky ignored his plea. "You're part of a gang and you didn't think I deserved to know that before I invited you into my *home*?"

She glared over Enzo's shoulder at Shaun. She blamed him for this, and he couldn't deny that it was entirely his fault. But if she wanted to know the truth, then she could have it.

Shaun held his hands up. "I'm not part of a bloody gang, all right?" he said with indignation. "I told you I got dragged into it too. The bit about Blackpool was all true, I promise you. I hate all of this. Honest I do."

Becky shook her head. "That makes it worse. You expect me to feel sorry for you but didn't mind bringing it to my door, or what's left of it. You are a fucking hypocrite."

That had not been his intention at all. He had to make her see that. He barged past Enzo to take her in his arms. But before he could even try, she slapped him hard across the face. Physically it was nothing compared to the blow he'd got earlier but it cut deeper. He liked Becky and could kick himself for what he'd done.

"Get out of my house," she shouted. "I never want to see either of you again."

Enzo pulled Shaun away from her and pushed him towards the staircase. "Enough," he said, putting his hand up. "Shaun, go downstairs. I mean it. Just go."

Shaun dithered and went to the top of the stairs, his face smarting from the slap and the embarrassment. A tear escaped his eye, but what was the use? He had brought mayhem to her quiet life and he couldn't even begin to defend himself. To do so would only make matters worse.

"If you mention this to anyone, police, friends, whoever, you will find yourself so far into this you won't get out," Enzo said to Becky. "Are you listening to me?"

A red-faced Becky nodded, rubbing her hand. "No need to worry. I know how this works." She sneered. "You can spare me the threats. I want nothing more to do with either of you. This is a quiet village with decent people in it. We don't need you infecting it. That man was right. You are scum."

Enzo nodded gravely. "Send a bill to the farm for the damages."

With that he turned on his heel and walked towards Shaun. "I told you, get downstairs," he ordered. "Move it."

As Enzo bundled him down the stairs, Shaun took a last look at Becky. Sheer venom exuded from her as she watched them go.

He hated what he had done to her. Her words would reverberate round his head for days to come. They were all the more cutting because they were true.

Downstairs, the house wasn't as bad as it had sounded. Thankfully, the door was still on its hinges and the clean-up would be more cosmetic than anything else. A couple of chairs lay in pieces and paintings smashed where those bastards had fought their way down the stairs.

"I came here to help her make this place better," Shaun said. "Instead, I brought carnage."

Enzo grabbed hold of him. "You could have been killed, you stupid fool."

Shaun allowed him to embrace him for a second before extracting himself. "We'd better get out of here. I don't fancy another slap."

They made their way outside and walked down the driveway in silence. Mercifully, the street lay deserted. For a village full of nosy people, Shaun thanked everything holy that none of them had come to see what the ruckus had been about. Across the road, Shaun saw a figure draw the curtains at Jean's. That must be Frank. He hoped his pay-out had been worth it.

"We should go," Enzo said. "We don't know who's around. I don't fancy a car chase tonight on top of everything else."

"I'm sorry," Shaun mumbled.

"I'm sure you are." Enzo sighed. "Aren't we all?"

Chapter Twelve

They drove through the village in silence. Shaun struggled to control his breathing, just like he'd learnt all those years ago on his travels. His yoga master had told him to live in the moment, but if Shaun had a choice, he would prefer to live in the past these days. The here and now didn't have much to offer him.

So much had happened just in the last half an hour. His body seemed to be rejecting it. He didn't think he would ever forget that face in the doorway. The enjoyment on the lad's face made Shaun's blood run cold. How could anyone get a kick out of violence? The lifestyle or the money he could almost understand, but that man had been desperate to get in the room with them. Then what would have happened? It didn't bear thinking about.

Once again, he found himself in a car next to Enzo, struggling to come to terms with another attempt on his life. This felt sickeningly familiar. His jaw throbbed where he'd been slapped but it was nothing compared to his ego. He'd had every right to be outraged about the incident at the Christmas markets. He didn't have that luxury this time. He had brought all of this on himself.

The car bumped over a pothole and jolted him back to life. His trouble wasn't over yet. In fact, the events at Becky's would be nothing once the truth got out at the farm. Once more he would be the weakest link of the chain.

"Will you tell Marco?" he asked.

Enzo considered it for a second. "It's going to be pretty hard to hide it."

The bright red mark on his neck where he'd almost been choked to death would be there for all to see. Shaun thought he might burst into tears.

"Your poor neck," he said miserably.

Even though he felt as low as a worm's tit, he desperately wanted to ask Enzo why he'd kissed him. But he couldn't bring himself to. Enzo glanced at him as they turned off the main road onto the farm track. If Shaun didn't know any better, the same question was on Enzo's mind too.

"You weren't to know," Enzo said.

Shaun reached over and placed his hand on Enzo's leg. "Thank you so much, Enzo. You seem to be making a habit of being my knight in shining armour. I do appreciate it and you."

Enzo looked at him but left it a fraction too long and the car veered off the track. They had quite a drop to the side so Enzo had to wrench the wheel to get the car away from it and back under control.

"Maybe we should talk about that another time," Enzo said.

"Good idea," Shaun replied.

Another near-death experience was absolutely not on his agenda. Although once Marco found out what had happened, even Enzo might have trouble defending him. Poor Liam had a one-way ticket to being caught in the middle of him and Marco once more and he didn't even know it yet.

Only minutes later, they parked up in the farmyard. Shaun felt like a condemned man. "Shit. Fuck," he exclaimed. "I'm supposed to be in my room."

What had he been thinking? Creeping out like a grounded teenager and going to his mate's to get drunk. He could see how ridiculous it had all been. These fixations of his had got him into bother all his life. The trouble was, he didn't seem to be in the market to learn by his mistakes.

"Come on," Enzo said softly. "Chances are Marco's in bed."

They were never going to be that lucky. Marco had obviously seen the car lights appear and come down to talk to Enzo about the night. When he saw a dejected Shaun come in followed by a bloody-necked Enzo, his face turned to thunder.

"Living room. Now," he barked, leading them down the hall.

Shaun followed. Whatever came next, he deserved it. He steeled himself for the inevitable. *Once more into the lounge to choke on humble pie.* For once in his life, he would really try to keep his stupid mouth shut and just take it.

As they entered the living room, Shaun took in all the decorations he and Enzo had put up. They were mocking him now and he wanted to smash them all to pieces. This bloody farm was going to be the death of him.

Instead of going on a one-man rampage, he slumped down on the couch, feeling very sorry for himself.

"What the fuck has been going on?" Marco asked. He perched on the edge of the chair and stared hard at Shaun.

"It's all my fault. I've been a dick," Shaun said, holding his hands up.

Marco looked up at Enzo, who stood uncertainly by the door.

"It's true. He has been a dick," Enzo said.

Shaun raised an eyebrow but bit back the temptation to make a response. A wisecrack now could very well be fatal.

"He went to some woman we met at yoga's house," Enzo blurted out.

Enzo had helped yet again, taking the burden of starting the conversation from him. Shaun had no idea how to form the words to express his ridiculous actions.

Marco glared at Shaun. "I thought you were in bed. What are you? Twelve?"

Again, Shaun swallowed down the words bubbling up inside him. In any other situation, he would be exceptionally proud of himself for such self-restraint, but he had no right at that moment.

"How did you get involved?" Marco asked Enzo. "Don't tell me you joined the fucking party."

"Two wankers turned up and tried to lift him," Enzo said.

Marco ran his hands over his face. "Oh Jesus Christ," he groaned. "This gets better. How did they know you were there? I suppose you put it on Facebook."

"Of course not," Shaun snapped. "You made me close my Facebook, remember? They had some local halfwit on the payroll. How was I to know that?"

Marco sprang up and paced across to Enzo. He examined his neck. "I suppose they gave you that?"

Enzo nodded.

"And the woman? What's to stop her going to the fucking police?"

"She won't," Shaun said, whirling round in his seat. "This scared the living shit out of her. Honestly, if we bung a bit of money her way, she won't talk."

Terrified, Shaun worried Marco would have a more permanent solution for Becky. Perhaps his paranoia had overruled his senses, but he had no idea the depths Marco would stoop to to please his uncle. He might not be Jonny Wellingham, but they all sipped from the same cup, didn't they?

"It's true, boss," Enzo said. "Then I added a warning for good measure. I don't think she'll talk."

Marco paced over to Shaun. "Well, that's something, I suppose. He's still out there, and yet again, you nearly give him what he wants. For fuck's sake, Shaun. That's it then. You've left me no choice. You're under house arrest."

Shaun leapt up so he was toe to toe with Marco. "You can fuck off. You can't keep me here against my will."

Marco grabbed hold of Shaun by the shirt. "Watch me. I am going to keep you alive if it kills me. You are Liam's brother, you selfish little bastard. I happen to love that man and I will not watch him go through losing you because you're a wanker. We will take it in shifts to check you are in the house, if that's what it takes. And don't get in my face, you've brought all of this on yourself."

He shoved Shaun so he fell against the sofa.

At that moment Liam, Claire, Dolly and Giovanni came in.

"Marco?" Liam asked, his face aghast. "What's going on now?"

Marco stormed through them towards the door. "Ask your brother," he shouted over his shoulder.

Liam scanned the room before running after Marco.

Enzo helped Shaun to his feet. "Are you okay?"

Shaun nodded.

"Well?" Giovanni asked, his arms folded. "Is anyone going to enlighten us? I guess it has something to do with you, Shaun."

"Oh, don't start," Shaun said wearily. "I've dealt with the organ grinder. Why don't you toddle off and wait until you're told?"

Giovanni darted towards Shaun, but Enzo blocked him. They were both heavily built but Enzo had the edge on Giovanni. His bulk easily protected Shaun.

"There's been enough of that tonight, brother," he said firmly. "Step back."

But Giovanni noticed Enzo's neck. "Who did that?" he demanded.

"It's my fault, all right?" Shaun replied. "That's what you want to hear, isn't it?"

"You?" Giovanni said, launching himself towards Shaun again.

But once more, Enzo got in the way. "It's not like that. He didn't do this. Don't be so ridiculous."

Shaun just wanted to be alone, the room and the stares of judgement stifling him. He barged past Enzo and Giovanni and ran out of the room. He didn't stop running until he got into his bedroom.

Why hadn't he just stayed in here?

Anxiety flooded his system. Pacing up and down in front of the bed, he cursed himself for his stupidity. He jumped out of his skin when the door opened. Dolly stood in the doorway like some Eighties soap star. He didn't have the energy for more confrontation.

"Dolly. Please leave me alone. I can't take it. I can't go over it again," Shaun cried, wringing his hands. He felt as though he were unravelling.

She rushed across the room and took him in her arms. "I've come for you, my love," she said, kissing the top of his head. "You don't have to talk."

The warmth from Dolly gave him comfort. Shaun's final defences came tumbling down. He burst into tears and let Dolly guide him to the end of the bed. They both sat and she held him close as he let the trauma he had been through that night escape him.

Shaun had no idea how long they sat there. It was clichéd, but time really stood still. Once Shaun's sobs had subsided, he and Dolly just sat there in silence.

Eventually he broke away and wiped his eyes with the back of his hand. "I bet I look like shit," he managed.

Dolly nodded. "Pretty much."

"Thank you," Shaun said, squeezing her hand. "I appreciate it."

"Any time, lad," she said with a smile. "We're in the same boat, you and me. Both dragged into this mess with no please or thank you. I think it only right we should stick together."

"At least you're part of it. I'm in some fucked-up no-man's-land with mops and potato peelers."

Dolly sighed. "I'm going to say something now and you're to hear me out. Do you understand?"

Shaun nodded. His trust in her at this point was true. She would sweeten the bitter medicine she was going to make him swallow. But he had a truth bomb coming his way and Dolly smoothed her skirt down as she readied herself.

"This is shit for everyone," she said calmly. "Well, except for Marco who's living his Tony Soprano fantasy. Anyway. I totally understand where you're coming from, but your behaviour is putting us all at risk."

Shaun went to say something, but Dolly whipped her hand out from his and put a finger over his lips. "I'm not done, thank you," she said firmly. "But I think everyone expecting you to be skivvy is not helping. So, we find you something to do."

"I'm not doing anything for gangs." Shaun pouted. "I've told Marco I do not approve of this life."

"There you go again, flying off the handle." Dolly sighed. "You don't bloody have to. Liam told me they're going to set you up in a yoga retreat or something? When all this shit is over."

"That's right. It's the least they can do," Shaun replied. He had a good mind to throw a week in the Caribbean into the equation after tonight.

"Then we get the ball rolling," Dolly said triumphantly.

This revelation stunned Shaun. To have a project like that would be perfect. It would make him feel that he had something to work towards. Then an idea struck him.

"I'm going to start a YouTube channel. If I can do some yoga things here and build up a following, they will come when we open."

Dolly slapped him on the leg. "That's the spirit. There's a lot of money online."

Then he slumped down. "But I don't have the equipment and I'm under house arrest. Even I wouldn't dare ask Marco for shore leave to set up a YouTube channel."

To his amazement, Dolly burst out laughing. "Don't you worry about that, love. Claire's got a load of gear at her flat. When it was the pandemic, we set her up online. Not quite yoga but she got in some positions, I can tell you."

Shaun grinned. It felt good. In fact, it felt amazing.

Then the idea that Enzo, downstairs arguing with his brother, might hear Shaun's laugh made him bury it down.

"There's something else?" Dolly asked, her smile also fading.

"It's Enzo," Shaun said. He couldn't keep it in any longer. "He kissed me."

Ever unshockable, Dolly didn't even blink. "And how did it feel?"

Once more a grin crept on Shaun's face. "Incredible. But it's the worst idea ever."

"Oh, they're the best kinds, love. Want to know a secret?"

Shaun nodded. He always wanted to know a secret.

"Me and Giovanni aren't strangers to each other's rooms either."

Genuinely shocked, Shaun reared back. "Are you kidding me?"

"No. It's bloody cold at night in this old shack. Why not?" She sniffed. "We're living day to day. No one knows how this is going to play out. I'm grabbing a bit of happiness where I can."

All of a sudden, the world seemed very different to Shaun.

Chapter Thirteen

He lay staring at the ceiling. The others had gone to bed hours ago. Shaun had listened as each one of them as they came up the stairs, but sleep eluded him. *A near-death experience, a kiss from a man you're starting to obsess over and a showdown with a gang boss will do that to you. Even if the gang boss is practically your brother-in-law and a caretaker boss.*

An owl hooted in the woods outside. He thought about his walk to Becky's. Had the lad from the village been in the woods? What if Wellingham's men had been there already? Shaun wouldn't be lying there now. At best he'd be in a basement somewhere and at worst… Well, he didn't even want to think about that.

The door handle turned slowly, as though whoever was on the other side didn't want to make any noise. Shaun sat bolt upright, his heart racing again. Were they in the house? Frantically, he grabbed the glass of water by his bed and readied to launch it at the door.

Slowly the door opened and there was Enzo, framed in the light from the hallway. Shaun let out a sigh.

"Fucking hell, you nearly gave me a heart attack," he gasped, putting the glass on the nightstand again.

He was getting quite adept at finding weapons in the unlikeliest of places. Not a skill he'd ever thought he would need.

Enzo slipped into the room and shut the door behind him. Now just lit by the moonlight coming in from the curtains Shaun hadn't bothered to close, he looked incredible, the intimacy of the moment sending Shaun's body into high alert.

"Sorry," Enzo whispered.

He stood there in just pyjama bottoms, his thick-set body covered in dark hair and solid muscle. He rubbed his arms from the cold.

"Here. Get in," Shaun said, pulling the duvet back.

Enzo hesitated for a second before diving under the covers. Their bodies didn't touch but Shaun could feel his heat. His cock instantly sprang to life.

"Is this a good idea?" Enzo asked.

"I think we're way past that now," Shaun replied.

Enzo settled himself against the pillow. They reminded Shaun of a couple from a sitcom he used to watch as a kid. They always shared a bed but never touched.

"And what can I do for you?" Shaun asked.

"I couldn't sleep," Enzo said. "I figured you'd be in the same boat."

They sat there for a second in silence. Shaun didn't know what to do next, but his body tingled at the fact he was under the duvet with this gorgeous man. Even if the silence between them had become slightly uncomfortable. It was like Enzo had used all his strength to get in the room and once there froze.

"You kissed me," Shaun said eventually.

Enzo shifted awkwardly. The duvet slipped from his chest to his waist, exposing that solid body again. The temptation to run his hands all over him became harder to fight. Shaun's hard cock would give him away. *Thank God for the duvet.*

"I did. I want to do it again, as well," Enzo whispered.

Shaun turned his face up and their lips touched, far less urgent than the kiss they'd shared after seeing off Wellingham's men. Gently, Shaun took Enzo's hand as they drank each other in.

Shaun flitted his tongue between Enzo's lips, who opened his mouth for him. Everything about Enzo gave him safety. Returning the favour, Enzo explored Shaun's mouth with his tongue. Once again, the connection with Enzo overwhelmed him. But for once, their lives weren't in danger. He gripped Enzo's huge biceps, desperate to feel them around him.

Underneath the duvet, his cock ached for contact. All he wanted to do was to straddle Enzo and take this to its logical conclusion, but something held him back.

"What is the matter?" Enzo asked with a frown as Shaun lay back on the pillow

"Marco told me about your lover. In Naples," Shaun replied. "You're vulnerable."

Enzo turned onto his side, his head resting on the pillow. Shaun matched him so they were facing.

Illuminated perfectly, Enzo looked so handsome Shaun's heart cried out for him.

"Carmine was… It was complicated," Enzo began.

"Marco told me he had a wife."

Enzo sighed, seemingly faraway for a second. "He did and we shouldn't have done it. But sometimes things can't be stopped."

Shaun reached out and took his hand. Shaun hadn't been immune to disastrous love affairs. In fact, he'd made a habit of leapfrogging from one to the other.

"When he was killed, I thought I'd never smile again," Enzo said. "That was why I was so quiet when I first got here. But spending time with you this last week has opened my eyes. I will never stop grieving for him, but he's gone."

"I know what you mean," Shaun said. "When Liam told me what happened to our mother, I thought I should be more upset. Liam was devastated when we sat in that hospital, but it felt numb to me. I think I always knew. Deep down."

"Carmine wasn't a fool. He knew the risks of this game. We all do," Enzo said, a tear escaping his eye. "But he also would never stand in the way of me finding happiness. You make me happy, Shaun. You drive me fucking crazy but you make me happy too."

The temptation had become way too strong. This course of action would probably get him in more trouble with Marco and he'd vowed to not be reckless. But he was only human.

"Want to know a secret?" Shaun said with a grin.

"Of course," Enzo replied.

"Your brother and Dolly are at it."

Enzo raised his head. "Really? He never said."

"Seems to me there are more secrets in this house than in MI5."

"Good for them," Enzo decided. "Come to me."

He opened his arms and Shaun scooted along the bed. Enzo wrapped him in an embrace and Shaun let out a sigh as their bodies touched.

"You may regret this in the morning," Shaun murmured, his mouth getting closer to Enzo's.

"Then we'll deal with that then," Enzo replied.

Shaun silenced him with a kiss. This time it was a hungry one, their tongues exploring each other's mouths and their hands roaming each other's bodies. Shaun ran his hands over Enzo's solid waist. He had wanted to explore this body ever since that day on the moors and he was quaking now that time had come.

Enzo ran his hand down Shaun's arm, leaving little tingles, until he reached the waistband of his boxer shorts. "Let me see you," he whispered.

Shaun dragged his boxers down. His cock stood proudly, and he moaned as Enzo took hold of him. Enzo's large hand encircled the head of Shaun's cock and he squeezed. God, it felt good. It had been quite some time since anyone had touched him, and that it was Enzo set Shaun's body on fire.

Taking control, Shaun pushed him back. He got up onto his knees and pulled at Enzo's pyjamas. As they slipped down, they revealed Enzo's thick, solid dick. It was everything Shaun had expected it to be...and it was all he could do to stop from dribbling.

"Fuck, you're incredible," Shaun whispered. He ran a hand down Enzo's chest, following his happy trail until he lightly stroked his cock. With the gentlest of touches, he traced around the head.

"So are you," Enzo soothed. "Come."

Shaun straddled Enzo, their cocks jostling together, making him forget the drama of the evening. Enzo kissed him harder, his tongue dancing against Shaun's. Enzo grabbed Shaun's hair and held his head in place. Shaun cupped Enzo's face with his hands.

He wished these kisses would never end. But he wanted to taste Enzo. He crawled down his body, placing kisses as he went. He rolled Enzo's hard nipple between his teeth, making him gasp and run his hand through Shaun's hair.

They were on the edge of a precipice and Shaun had no option but to dive over.

He took hold of Enzo's cock at the base and guided it into his mouth. He slid his lips down the hard shaft, making Enzo's body stiffen.

"Shaun," he murmured.

Shaun could smell shower gel and musky scent combined. Sucking hard, he ran his tongue down the protruding vein. Enzo let out a small cry.

They would have to be quiet and Shaun didn't know if he would be able to once Enzo returned the favour. His dick needed attention, but he couldn't stop driving Enzo's cock in and out of his mouth.

Panting, he looked up at Enzo, who returned his stare. Shaun licked the tip of Enzo's cock, the faint taste of precum making him all the hornier.

Sitting up, Enzo took hold of Shaun's face and raised him up for another kiss. Shaun grabbed hold of Enzo's shoulders for balance. Their bodies melded together as they explored each other's mouths. The relief of finally being in Enzo's arms made Shaun want to shout from the rooftops. Despite the events of the evening, everything felt perfect.

Enzo laid Shaun back so his head was at the foot of the bed. Spreading his legs wide, Shaun gave himself up to whatever sensation Enzo had in mind for him. He was more than happy to relinquish all power to him.

Gently, Enzo traced the outline of Shaun's dick with the tip of his finger. Every time he made contact, electricity shot up Shaun's spine. Just the mere touch of this man sent him into another realm.

Shifting into position, Enzo kissed Shaun's dick. Enzo's breath made Shaun quiver. He desperately wanted the warmth that Enzo's mouth would bring.

Enzo didn't keep him waiting for long. He engulfed Shaun's cock with his mouth and Shaun had to bury his face in the scrunched-up duvet to stop the cries from waking the house.

Sucking hard, Enzo tugged at Shaun's balls. This was on a level he had never experienced. Enzo worked Shaun's cock with unbridled hunger, making his whole body tense. Enzo let Shaun's cock fall out of his mouth and sucked at his balls. They contracted at his touch. Enzo flicked his tongue over one, then the other.

"Oh God, that feels good," Shaun whispered.

Suddenly Enzo lifted Shaun's legs, exposing his arse. Enzo traced his tongue along the skin separating it from his balls. More tingles shot through Shaun's body. Then Enzo's tongue made contact with Shaun's hole. This time he did cry out. He tried not to, but the way that Enzo was working his body, it was impossible.

Enzo moved him into a position where he could get better access. Shaun wriggled in ecstasy as Enzo lapped away at him—long, powerful strokes that sent him into orbit each time. All the tension of the last few hours evaporated as Shaun gave himself up to the ride.

Eventually, his hole slick with Enzo's spit, Shaun lowered his legs. Enzo smiled at him. Shaun thought his heart would break at how connected they were in that moment. All those conversations, arguments and laughs had led up to right now.

Reaching between his legs, Enzo slowly pushed his finger inside Shaun. At first his arse clenched, fighting against Enzo's thick finger.

"Just relax," Enzo whispered.

Shaun let his body flop and Enzo probed deeper inside him. With his other hand, Enzo massaged Shaun's cock.

"I'll come," Shaun whispered.

"That's the point," Enzo replied.

Powerless to do anything else, Shaun gave in to the undulating sensations as Enzo manipulated him with both hands. They never broke eye contact.

The moment came from nowhere.

"Fuck, I'm going to come," Shaun cried.

Enzo tugged at his cock harder. "Come on, Shaun. Show me," he said.

Shaun arched his back and tightened the grip of his hole around Enzo's finger that pressed hard on his prostate.

At that moment, with pleasure invading every one of his senses, Shaun knew he was falling in love with Enzo. It terrified him and excited him all at once. But then all thoughts were out of his head as the orgasm ripped through his system.

The waves overcame him so he was floating on air. He arched his back and gripped the sheets as the exquisite pain rushed through him. His body was wracked with aftershocks as Enzo gently coaxed every last drop out of him. Opening his eyes, Shaun saw Enzo slicking his own cock with Shaun's cum.

"You are so fucking sexy," Enzo said.

Leaning over him, Enzo balanced with one hand while he pulled feverishly with the other. "Oh God, I'm going to come, Shaun."

Shaun luxuriated in the hot, sticky spurts of cum that rained down on him as Enzo screwed his face up. "Oh fuck, yeah," Enzo managed.

Shaun watched the pleasure pass over Enzo's face. He stroked Enzo's leg which twitched as Enzo came slowly back to life. "Towel?" he asked, leaning down to kiss Shaun.

"On the side," Shaun said.

Planting a kiss on Shaun's forehead, Enzo rolled off the bed and retrieved it. He cleaned himself up and threw it down for Shaun, who did the same. To Shaun's amazement, Enzo got on the bed and reached his arm across the pillow for Shaun to join him.

"Are you staying with me?" Shaun asked.

"My love, I'm staying with you every night until you tell me not to," Enzo replied.

Shaun scooted up the bed and snuggled into Enzo. He kissed his chest, tasting the salty sweat.

"That's a dangerous deadline, my friend," Shaun said. "I may never tell you not to."

At last, Enzo wrapped him in his arms. Those thick, strong arms gave him all the protection he had dreamed they would.

"That is fine with me." Enzo murmured.

There was plenty of time for talk about the future tomorrow. Tonight, Shaun wanted to fall asleep and wake up still wrapped against the body of this wonderful man.

Chapter Fourteen

Shaun did wake entwined with Enzo. He felt secure—a feeling he hadn't had since Harry had come barging into the bed and breakfast all those months ago. It was a welcome relief. Even if it was temporary.

Enzo's breath tickled the back of his neck as he snored gently. It had been inevitable that they would end up here. Shaun didn't regret a thing. In fact, he only regretted that they didn't get here sooner. However, he also knew the value of keeping things secret and it wouldn't be long before the house started waking up.

He thought about Dolly and Giovanni, probably snuggled up together like this in another room, just along the landing. He marvelled at how they'd managed to keep it a secret. However, he suspected his big mouth would probably be the reason why the others would find out about him and Enzo.

If only they could lock the door and wait out this period in their lives, wrapped together away from harm.

"What time is it?" Enzo whispered.

"Coming up to seven," Shaun answered, glancing at the clock on the nightstand.

"The day will begin soon."

Shaun squeezed his arm and kissed it. "Give it ten minutes."

He wanted to hold the cold winter morning at bay a little longer. The heat of their bodies melded together was too comforting to give up easily.

"I don't think we should let anyone know about this," Enzo said.

He agreed, but after spending the night with Enzo, he wanted to shout it from the rooftops. The first glimmer of happiness in months would be hard to keep under control.

"Marco is strung out enough," he managed. "And I would like to get through one day without being screamed at. So yes, I agree."

Enzo chuckled, his deep timbre making Shaun's neck vibrate.

"You are overplaying the Cinderella act a little," he whispered. "You have some work to do after last night."

The events of the night before rushed over him again. Enzo was right. Shaun had been totally out of line, but today he would show the whole house that he was a changed man. This time he would not fail.

"You'd better go," he said. "I can't be Mr Prim and Proper if the others get wind of this."

Enzo didn't move. "I think we need to straighten out what this is. I can't spend the day wondering."

The big question had arrived sooner than Shaun had expected. It came as a blessing though. Shaun would have spent the day stressing. He didn't do uncertainty. It made him anxious. Hence why he'd found the last few months absolutely unbearable. Shaun liked to be in control of the rudder.

"We can't make any promises to each other," he replied. "Dolly is right. We all need to get through this. Then we can see. It won't be long, surely."

Enzo squeezed him tighter. "Uncle will be here in the new year. It's only a few weeks at most. I think you're right. Anyway, I quite like having a night-time rendezvous. It's exciting. Makes it just for us. Giovanni would want to know everything. He's not your biggest fan, in case you hadn't noticed."

"I'd got the gist of that," Shaun muttered. "You've got a bigger cock though."

"What?"

Shaun giggled. "When he came into the bathroom, I got an eyeful. I thought you should know that yours is bigger."

"Don't tell him that, for fuck's sake," Enzo replied. "Are you sure though?"

"Positive."

Enzo pressed his cock against Shaun's body. "I like that," he whispered.

Shaun stroked his arm. "Will you come tonight?"

Enzo kissed the back of his neck. He had quickly learnt last night that it was a sensitive part of Shaun's body and capitalised on it.

"Try stopping me."

Shaun turned in his arms. Their lips met and Enzo's hand crept down to his ass cheek.

Reluctantly, Shaun reached down and removed it.

"You're going to start something you can't finish," he murmured.

Enzo kissed the tip of his nose. "I will finish it later. You have my promise on that one."

He got out of the bed making absolutely no effort to hide his erection. Shaun salivated over the forbidden fruit.

"You're a bad man, Enzo," he said with a chuckle.

Enzo rubbed his cock and looked Shaun in the eye. "I don't know what you mean."

* * * *

Shaun laid the bacon on a plate and put it in the centre of the table. Liam, Marco, Giovanni and Claire all dove straight for it.

"I thought we had no food in," Giovanni asked, munching on a rasher before it even got to his plate.

"I found some in the freezer last night, didn't I?" Shaun asked, sipping his coffee.

"More like you fed us that shite to teach us a lesson," Claire muttered.

Shaun winked. "No comment."

Dolly came in, looking very refreshed. "Something smells good," she said, sitting down. "I'm starving."

"I think we all have an appetite this morning," Shaun said.

Dolly caught his eye, but he didn't dare grin even though that was all he wanted to do. He needed to be meek and sorrowful today or Marco would be after his blood again.

"Where's Enzo?" Claire asked.

"In the shower," Giovanni said. "He's slow this morning."

This time Shaun busied himself opening another packet of bacon. Dolly would be scanning him for clues as to what went on last night. She would have to wait. He had something else to deal with first and he wanted to get it over with before Enzo came down. He really didn't want him to witness his discomfort. Giovanni having a front-row seat was bad enough.

"Marco. I want to apologise again," he said. "What I did last night was fucking stupid and I promise you, it won't happen again."

The room fell silent. All eyes were on Marco. Liam placed his hand on Marco's arm and nodded.

Marco sighed. "It is accepted but if you think a bit of bacon and a sorry is going to lift your house arrest, think again."

Shaun sat next to Marco. "I understand. I've brought it on myself. You won't get any fight from me."

Raising his eyebrow, Marco peered at him. "You have changed your tune."

"A boy can, can't he?" Shaun sniffed. "I did a lot of thinking last night. I'm totally ashamed of myself."

But Marco could not be fooled so easily. "Something else is happening here. What do you need, Shaun?"

For a young man he was very perceptive. Once he got control of his impulsive nature, he would be a wonderful leader. If only he led anything other than a bloody gang.

Before he could speak, Dolly cleared her throat.

"The lad is worth more than being our glorified servant," she said, squeezing ketchup onto her bacon sandwich. "So, he's going to launch his own yoga channel. We discussed it all last night. It's a bloody good idea."

Marco had his own sandwich halfway to his mouth when he froze. "His what? I can't leave any of you alone for five bloody minutes."

"A YouTube channel," she said as if it was the most natural thing in the world. "He can use the dining room."

Totally confused, Marco frowned at Shaun. "Please elaborate. Make it quick. We have a shit ton of things to do today and already I have a blinding headache."

His moment had come and he wasn't going to blow it. He had absolutely no right to ask any favours of Marco, but Shaun had enough about him to at least try.

"If the offer is still open for a yoga retreat, and believe me I will understand if it's not, but if it is... Well, I thought I could do it right here and build up followers. It'll create a buzz and I can hit the ground running when I finally get to wherever I'm going," he blurted out.

Marco bit into his sandwich and chewed slowly. Claire and Liam seemed to be transfixed by their plates. Shaun could well imagine the steely look on Dolly's face, but he didn't dare turn and see.

"Seems like a pretty good idea to me," Giovanni said.

Shaun's jaw dropped, which made him wince from the punches he'd received the night before. Even so, he did not expect support to come from that corner. He had been pretty rough on Giovanni. He suspected that Dolly had spoken to him...but didn't want to know what methods she'd used to talk Giovanni around.

Marco slowly replaced his sandwich on the plate and shook his head. "I miss everything that goes on in this house. I have half a mind to start a sharing session at breakfast. Then you can tell me all the schemes you've cooked up when I dare go to sleep and I don't have to worry."

At that point, Enzo came in looking absolutely gorgeous with his hair still wet and a white T-shirt on that clung to his slightly damp body. Flashbacks of everything they had got up to the night before ran through Shaun's mind like a cinema reel. But he couldn't be distracted. He needed to focus.

"What?" Enzo asked. "What's been going on?"

"Chill out," Claire replied, pushing a chair out for him with her foot. "Shaun is telling us how he wants to be the next Jane Fonda."

Enzo's shoulders slumped and he sat next to Giovanni. "Oh right."

Shaun leapt up and poured him a coffee from the machine. Not catching his eye once, he set the cup before him then returned to his seat. This time he did see Dolly's probing gaze. A glint of amusement in her eye told him they'd been rumbled.

"Well?" he asked. He even managed to muster a hopeful smile.

"Fine," Marco said. "It can't hurt. Wellingham knows where we are anyway. But I'm watching you."

"That's the idea," Shaun said. "Although I didn't have you down as a yoga fan. Perhaps you and Liam could take up tantric sex."

"And you're still in the doghouse," Marco added, ignoring his last comment. "Don't get too carried away."

"Bloody hell, I've said I'm sorry. What more do you want?"

Marco winked at a worried Liam. "Let me think. I know how you can redeem yourself to all of us. Your roast beef dinner with all the trimmings could tip the scales in your favour."

"A Sunday roast? But it's Tuesday," Claire said. "You Italians are crazy, man."

The table burst into much-needed laughter, the atmosphere lifting and everyone visibly relaxing.

"You've got yourself a deal," Shaun said. "But can someone please go to the bloody supermarket today?"

Enzo had finished loading two slices of bread with the rest of the bacon. "I'll do it." He bit into the sandwich. Grease dripped down his chin. Shaun had to fight the urge to dab it for him. They were all back on an even keel. Things did not need disrupting again with Marco finding out Shaun had slept with his cousin.

"Can you give me a lift into town?" Claire asked. "Jessie is renting one of those new flats down by the river and the bloody landlord has got wind of why. He's into religion and has gone batshit crazy."

Marco frowned. "How?"

"I don't know, do I?" she answered. "That's why I need to go down. She's threatening to sock him one. Some of the names he called her weren't very Christian."

Thinking about it, Marco turned to Giovanni. "You go as well. I don't like this. If Wellingham is after us, it could be a trap. He'll be pissed that he failed again last night."

Giovanni nodded.

"We can run round by my place too," Claire said. "I'll get that equipment for you."

Shaun couldn't take his eyes off Enzo. He was so sexy Shaun wanted to launch himself over the table right then and there.

"Shaun?" Claire said.

He broke out of the moment. "Oh thanks. I'll get sorting the dining room out. I'll just go and have a shower first."

Enzo caught his eye as he got up.

Once in his room, he stared at the bed. He had to get a hold of himself. Before he could even attempt it, the door was flung open, and Enzo stood there.

Wordlessly, they crashed together. They kissed hard and Enzo pushed him down so he sat on the end of the bed.

Crouching between his legs, Enzo glanced up at him. "You've got to stop looking at me like that," he panted. "I had a hard-on at the table."

"Like me now?" Shaun asked.

Enzo pulled at his trousers and boxers, so they were soon round his ankles. "You are so wonderful," he said.

He engulfed Shaun's cock with his lips and started to suck. Shaun fell onto the bed and gave himself up to the sensation.

Enzo worked him hard and Shaun reached behind him, grabbing the pillow and putting it over his face. "Oh fuck," he groaned into it.

In no time, he was coming, his cum spilling out of him into Enzo's mouth. The cool air hit him as he opened his eyes and removed the pillow. Enzo had licked his cock clean and sat on his haunches.

"Come here," Shaun said. He was more than ready to return the favour.

But Enzo shook his head. "I will buy condoms at the supermarket," he said. "Until then, I will wait."

Chapter Fifteen

The view from the top field was awe-inspiring. The valley stretched far below, and Shaun could see a church spire reaching through the winter mist. It looked like a Christmas card. He wished he could see it when it snowed. It would be so beautiful.

To fill his lungs with fresh country air felt good. Although they hadn't had much else in the last three months, after years of Blackpool's odour of fish and chips and cigarettes, Shaun didn't take it for granted.

"Wow," he said.

"Wow indeed," Liam replied.

Shaun smiled at his brother. He could still see that sad little boy in there if he looked really carefully. But a new, confident and vibrant young man had almost fully replaced him. It made Shaun's heart dance with joy.

"What?" Liam asked.

"You're growing into a decent man, Liam. I'm proud of you."

Liam reddened. "Shut up."

"I mean it," Shaun said with a grin. "While I was banging around like the oldest adolescent in Lancashire, you've turned into this. Mum would be so pleased."

Liam's eyes filled up a little at the mention of their mother. "She'd be too pissed to even notice. Oh, and she'd be cadging free drugs off me for her and her cronies."

Shaun laughed bitterly. "It's funny because it's true."

"It wasn't all bad though. Was it?" Liam asked.

Typical of him to still want to find the good stuff. They coped with the same things in such different ways.

"No, not all bad," he said. "Hey, do you remember that time—I think it was your birthday—Mum took us to Chester Zoo?"

Liam looked lost in thought. "Oh God yeah. She was with Barry then and he drove us in that clapped-out car of his. A right bloody death trap."

"You were obsessed with the penguins," Shaun said, lost in the memory of little Liam at the zoo. "You cried blue murder when we went to see something else. You spent the rest of the day banging on about the damn things."

"I remember you buying me a cuddly toy one at the gift shop," Liam said.

Shaun had a slightly different memory of that. "You *say* buy..."

Liam's mouth dropped open. "You pinched it?"

"You were driving me fucking mad. A boy can only listen to 'I want Pingu' so many times before he has to take matters into his own hands."

They made their way down the field towards the farmhouse. God forbid Shaun step one foot off the property. He had accepted his punishment of being stuck at the farm for the time being, but to have something to focus on could be the making of him. Even Marco couldn't complain about that.

"You little sod. Mum used to tell me all the time that you'd saved up your pocket money for that thing," Liam said.

"Wonder what happened to it," Shaun replied.

"It was at the flat," Liam said sadly. "It'll be long gone."

It touched Shaun that Liam had kept it all these years. Hard years where he hadn't had a fixed abode or any certainty, but he'd kept that raggedy old thing.

"It's times like this I miss her the most," Liam continued, quietly. "She'd be well chuffed we were together. Even like this. You were always her favourite. She should have stopped at one kid."

Shaun put his arm around his brother and drew him close. "You don't know that," he said. "She was a lot further gone when you came around. Everything had taken a hold."

The highs with his mother had been so much fun to a child. She hadn't been like other people's mums. She never nagged them about homework or bedtime. But the lows were intense. Some days she didn't get out of bed. Shaun got used to making him and Liam breakfast before school.

"I do speak to her sometimes, you know. When I'm alone," Shaun said. "I tell her how wonderful you are and that you're trying your best to find happiness."

"Me too," Liam replied. "I'm definitely telling her you nicked Pingu."

Shaun squeezed his shoulder. "It's hard, isn't it? Fucking Jonny Wellingham."

A hard, angry glare replaced the shy look on Liam's face. "He'll pay for it. Don't you worry about that."

This side of Liam, Shaun didn't like. It reminded him that he'd left him to the mercy of a gangland leader all those years ago. An act he would feel eternally guilty about. But he'd been young himself and grieving. "I should have taken you with me when I went travelling," he said, voicing his thoughts.

"Don't start that again," Liam said. "I wouldn't have gone. I thought Jonny and Harry were my family. We needed some space from each other."

Shaun supposed Liam was right. Shaun had taken on responsibility for Liam as soon as their mother disappeared but by the time Liam had left school, Shaun needed to get out. They each had processed their childhood in different ways.

"Don't get me wrong. I'm not happy about your life. I'm certainly not impressed I've been landed slap bang in the middle, but I'm glad about one thing," Shaun said.

"What's that?" Liam asked.

"That we've connected again."

"I am happy, you know," Liam said. "Marco is everything I've ever dreamed of."

Shaun grinned. "I bet he is."

"Not like that," Liam said, reddening. "Although he isn't shabby in that department either. But I love him, Shaun. Like, really love him."

It made Shaun's heart dance to hear his brother being so open about his feelings. As a child, he had locked them away. If Marco had helped Liam to be his true self, then they had Shaun's blessing. Shaun desperately wanted to tell his brother that he had exactly the same feelings for Enzo, but he couldn't.

He'd promised Enzo they would keep it on the downlow.

"Marco is lucky his uncle lets him be who he wants to be," Shaun said. "There's plenty in that world that wouldn't."

"Yeah, like Jonny fucking Wellingham," Liam said with a sneer. "Harry told me he had one of his original members shot because he was gay."

Shaun stopped walking. "What?"

Liam kicked a stone from the grass. "Yup. Harry guessed about me and Marco just before I ran for it. He told me about Lorenzo de Luca."

"Lorenzo de Luca?" Shaun exclaimed. "Fucking hell, how did they not know he was gay with a name like that?"

"I'm serious, Shaun," Liam said. "Him, Harry and Jonny were in the old gang together and they both helped Jonny take over. They were close as fuck. Then one day Jonny worked it out and had him shot. They dumped his body in the Mersey."

Shaun shivered. How could he have let his brother stay with a pig like that? He hadn't known how deep Jonny's cruel streak ran. Thank God he'd never worked out about Liam. It didn't bear thinking about.

"And I bet Harry pulled the trigger," Shaun replied. "Fucking lap dog."

They resumed walking.

"I don't think so," Liam said. "He could have handed me over to Jonny then and there. I know he didn't do anything to help in Dolly's flat, but when he told me about this Lorenzo guy, he was gutted. Even though it was fifteen years ago."

Shaun snorted. "Don't tell me you're feeling sorry for bloody Harry now."

"Course not, but he was all right when we were in Blackpool. He could have just finished us both off and been done with it."

Harry was an enigma to Shaun, but he had enough to think about with the gang he shared a house with, never mind the one trying to finish them all off. Anyone who helped Wellingham had to be stopped. Shaun might not be able to help on the frontline, but he would do everything in his power now to help.

If he thought worrying about keeping Liam safe was too much, now he'd added Enzo to the mix. If Wellingham and his mob were out of the picture, the mist would clear. He and Enzo could see if what they had was real and tangible. Shaun hoped desperately that it was.

They walked the rest of the way in silence, Shaun enjoying being side by side with his younger brother. No matter what happened with Enzo or even the yoga retreat, he didn't want Liam to be adrift from him again.

Once in the farmyard, Liam headed over to the barn.

"Where are you going?" Shaun called after him.

"Marco wanted me to check the hatch," Liam explained.

Shaun ran to catch up with him and they went into the barn. Enzo and Giovanni's gym equipment had been dumped everywhere.

"It's a right bloody mess in here," Shaun declared, pulling a face.

"Tell your bodyguard."

Shaun had already hatched a plan to offer to help Enzo clear it up. The things he could do to him on those gym mats made his cock surge. He couldn't wait until nightfall.

They headed over to the corner of the building. Nothing seemed to be out of place, although it was hard to tell. The elderly farmer had left a load of crates and what appeared to be an old cartwheel. Everything had been covered in bird shit. Perhaps this wasn't the location for a midnight assignation. Sometimes things should stay in one's head.

Shaun went to investigate further when Liam grabbed his arm. "Shaun. Look."

The window had a pane that had been smashed. The glass was on the floor inside the barn, so it had been done from outside.

"Who the fuck has done that?" Liam exclaimed.

A shiver ran down Shaun's spine. "I think we should tell Marco. Come on."

They half walked, half ran into the house.

"Marco?" Liam called. "Marco!"

Marco appeared in the lounge doorway. Once more, worry was etched on his face. All thoughts of broken windows and abandoned equipment left Shaun. "Something's happened," he said. "Hasn't it?"

"What is it?" Liam demanded.

"It was a fucking trap," Marco announced.

Enzo's in danger. "Where are they?" Shaun demanded.

"Where's who?" Dolly asked, coming in from having a smoke outside. "What is it?"

"The others are under fire," Marco said grimly.

"Under fire?" Shaun yelped. "You never said anything about being under fire!"

Dolly put her hand in his. "They'll be all right. They've been to this rodeo before, love. Marco, what are they doing?"

Marco ran his hands through his hair. Liam was instantly at this side, his arm around him.

"They're coming back," Marco said. "Enzo wanted to try and lose them, but I said not to bother. If we learnt anything by your moonlight flit, Shaun, it's that they know where we are."

Shaun sank down on a chair. Someone could be firing at Enzo at that very moment. He fought the anxiety rising in his system. Dolly sat next to him and rubbed his back. He realised she was in exactly the same position as him. She would be terrified for Giovanni.

Liam paced up and down. "I can't lose Claire," he said. "Marco. We must be able to do something."

But Shaun knew as well as everyone else that they could do absolutely nothing but wait.

Chapter Sixteen

They sat in the kitchen for what seemed like an age. Shaun refreshed the cafetiere twice and Dolly threatened to wear a tread in the kitchen floor by constantly going outside to smoke. The early winter dusk came and went, leaving only dark night.

As Shaun poured Marco yet another cup, Dolly burst through the door.

"There are lights on the track," she gasped.

"Wait," Marco instructed. "We don't know it's them." He dashed into the lounge and came out holding a gun. It turned Shaun's stomach, but he knew better than to say anything. By the time they were in the farmyard, the car had pulled up. *Enzo's BMW.* Shaun thanked everything holy.

Enzo scrambled out of the car. "Help me. He's been hit," he shouted to no one in particular.

Shaun dashed forward and met Enzo at the back door. A shaken Claire got out of the passenger side to be met by a bear hug from Liam.

"Are you okay?" Shaun whispered to Enzo who just shook his head.

They yanked the door open. Giovanni lay on the back seat, writhing in pain.

"Giovanni," Dolly shouted. "Can you hear me?"

"Of course, I can bloody hear you," Giovanni grumbled. "Your shouting would wake the dead. It's not that bad. I don't think it went in."

Enzo and Shaun helped Giovanni out. His light blue jeans were soaked in blood.

"Get him inside," Marco instructed.

With an arm on each shoulder, Enzo and Shaun supported Giovanni as he hobbled into the house.

"Where do you want him?" Enzo asked.

"Not in the lounge. We'll never get blood out of that carpet," Shaun said without thinking. He saw the others staring at him. "Sorry."

They settled on the kitchen table. Liam grabbed their coffee things as Enzo and Shaun got him comfortable.

"Does he need a hospital?" Claire asked.

"No hospital," Giovanni said. "Doll, see if you can see anything."

Dolly rolled her sleeves up. Nothing seemed to faze this woman. Then, he supposed she had lived in this world for most of her life. She'd probably seen it all and then some.

Tentatively, they lowered Giovanni's blood-soaked trousers. He had a deep gash in his thigh, but it was obviously not a bullet hole. They all sighed a collective sigh of relief.

"It's nicked you," Dolly said, peering around. "We'll get this cleaned up in no time. Shaun, love, get me a big bowl of water. Liam, run up to my room. I've got wipes and a bandage in my bedside drawer."

Liam made for the door before Dolly looked up. "Second drawer down," she shouted. "Don't go in the top one whatever you do." She winked at Giovanni.

Fifteen minutes and a lot of complaining from Giovanni later, Dolly had cleaned and bandaged his leg. "Come on, my love," she soothed. "Let's get you on that sofa."

Giovanni allowed her to help him off the table and down the corridor to the lounge.

"Are they…?" Claire asked.

Enzo nodded.

"Bloody hell," Claire continued, accepting the stiff gin that Shaun had poured her. "It's like being back in one of Wellingham's knocking shops round here."

Marco frowned. "Meaning?"

Claire sneaked a glance at Enzo then put her head down. "Just them two at it and you two."

He definitely didn't believe her. Shaun made a mental note to tackle Enzo on this. Had their secret already got out? It wouldn't surprise him.

Speaking of Enzo, ever since Giovanni had been given the all-clear, he hadn't said a word. He perched on the window seat, watching them all fussing over his brother. Shaun sat next to him. He really wanted to take him in his arms and whisper words of comfort in his ear, but instead he opted for a shoulder nudge. "You okay?"

"I am. Bit of a rough day."

"Are there any other kind round here?"

Liam finished cleaning the kitchen table and threw the cloth in the bucket. "You say he had you outnumbered?" he asked Claire.

"There was fucking loads of them."

"How many?"

"Easily fifteen, maybe twenty," she replied. "Enzo?"

Enzo rubbed his face. "I'd say nearer twenty."

"Shit," Marco said. "Where the hell did they come from?"

"Someone's helping him, but who?" Liam mused.

They sat in silence for a second, contemplating what this latest development meant for them. Then Shaun remembered why he and Liam had been dashing into the house.

"Marco. I don't want to lay any more shit on you, but Liam and I found broken glass in the barn."

Marco whirled around. "Broken glass?"

"Yeah," Liam added. "Someone's taken a windowpane out. From the outside."

"Fuck," Marco replied. "Do you reckon someone has been scoping us out?"

Liam nodded. "I don't like it. I've done this for him in the past."

It felt as though a net had tightened on them. How had Wellingham done this? The idea that the farm no longer kept them safe was too much to bear and terror coursed through Shaun's body once more.

* * * *

That night, Shaun lay in bed, feeling a mixture of excitement and nerves. He didn't know if Enzo would even come tonight. After the events of the day, it might be the last thing he would want.

An hour passed and still no sign of him. Perhaps he had been too obvious earlier or that Claire had clearly worked out that something was going on had put him off. He hadn't thought that Enzo would leave him hanging like this though. He deserved slightly better, but poor Enzo had been through so much, Shaun could forgive him for wanting to rest.

He heard that magical sound of the door handle being slowly turned. Shaun sat up and smoothed the covers down around him.

Enzo slipped into the room. Still fully clothed, he looked stressed out. Shaun couldn't wait to get him in the bed and his arms around him. He'd been wanting to do that for hours. "I was beginning to think you'd had second thoughts," he whispered.

"No way," Enzo said, unbuttoning his shirt. "Marco wanted to talk things through. I couldn't get away."

He flung the shirt onto a chair in the corner of the room. Once again, Shaun drank in his muscle-toned body. Anticipation flooded his system and he had to fight to keep from drooling.

"Are you naked under there?" Enzo asked, an amused grin appearing.

"Certainly am," Shaun said.

He moved the duvet a little, exposing the side of his body.

"Fuck," Enzo said, undoing his jeans and palming his cock in the process.

He let them fall to the floor and stepped out of them. That left him in just a pair of black boxer shorts. His cock, already solid, strained against the confines of the underwear. Shaun's own dick was as hard as a bullet as he watched his own personal strip show.

He reached under the duvet and squeezed himself. He couldn't wait much longer.

Enzo teased the waistband on his underwear. "You want something from me?" he asked with a grin.

Shaun kicked the covers off. "Too fucking right, I do."

Enzo's underwear was history and he fell on top of Shaun, who wrapped his legs around his waist. Their bodies fitted together perfectly, and running his hands up Enzo's back, Shaun revelled in every muscle.

God, he was so sexy, and feeling the weight of him only made Shaun all the hornier, if that were possible.

They kissed and Enzo's hard cock rubbed against Shaun's hole. He hoped to God he had managed to buy condoms before everything kicked off. Even for Shaun it had been inappropriate to ask before then.

They rolled over so Shaun straddled him. He leaned back, enjoying Enzo taking in his body. He might not be as hulking as his lover but he had a toned, lithe body that he was proud of. Enzo reached up and ran his fingers along Shaun's torso until he reached low enough to run his fingertips over Shaun's erection.

They never broke eye contact as Enzo rubbed the head. This was more than just sex. The connection between them made Shaun's heart race. He moved down and took Enzo's cock in his mouth. The salty precum on the tip exploded on his tongue, and Enzo groaned, spurring him on. Shaun needed no encouragement though. He could suck this forever.

But he had more in mind than blow jobs tonight. He sought out Enzo's lips. They kissed and Enzo rolled him over onto his back again.

He crouched between Shaun's legs and glanced up at him. "You are beautiful, Shaun," he whispered.

Not waiting for a reply, he leant down and took Shaun's cock between his lips. Shaun's body was electric at the heat over his dick. Enzo sucked him steadily, squeezing his balls with a free hand. Then he lifted Shaun's legs up and trailed his tongue down to Shaun's hole. He licked and teased, making Shaun groan. When Enzo came up for air, he pressed against Shaun's ass with his finger.

"Please tell me you got condoms and lube," Shaun whined.

"And if I did?" Enzo asked, a cheeky glint in his eye.

"If you did, then fuck me."

Nodding, Enzo leaned over and produced the essential items from his jeans pocket. Never had Shaun been so glad to see anything. His arse cried out for Enzo's cock. He hadn't been able to focus on anything all day.

Enzo fiddled with the packets. Usually, Shaun found this part of sex a mood killer, but watching the muscles in Enzo's body contract as he moved mesmerised Shaun. Lazily, he played with his cock until Enzo rolled a condom on his own. Squeezing a liberal amount of lube on his fingers, he ran them once more over Shaun's hole, the cool liquid making him start.

Then Enzo slipped a finger inside him, and Shaun flung his head back. God, it felt good. Enzo explored inside him, expertly stretching his hole.

"More," Shaun whispered.

Enzo eased a second finger inside Shaun, who clenched, getting used to the exquisite invasion. "Is that okay?" Enzo murmured.

"Fuck me, please," he replied. "I can't wait much longer."

Enzo nodded and slid his fingers out. Immediately, the big head of his cock pressed against Shaun. He spread his legs wider, his hunger for Enzo raging out of control.

The head breached Shaun's hole and Enzo entered him. For a split second, Shaun thought he wasn't going to be able to take such a big dick, but his body was faithful to him. Enzo slid all the way inside him, holding his legs in position.

They stayed there for a second, Shaun revelling in the way Enzo absolutely filled him.

"Ready?" Enzo asked.

Shaun nodded. Talk about an understatement. He'd been ready for this since the night before.

Enzo bucked his hips and began to slowly fuck Shaun. It seemed he was as worked up as Shaun as he didn't linger on a slow build-up but fucked him hard. It took Shaun's breath away and he grabbed the headboard.

Then Enzo dropped his pace and withdrew slowly until his cock was just on the edge before plunging it in again. Shaun let out a moan. God, this man had skills.

Pressing Shaun's knees against his chest, Enzo leaned forward and kissed him.

"Oh fuck, Enzo," he managed when Enzo pulled back.

"Get on your hands and knees," Enzo instructed.

Shaun obliged and gasped into the pillow as Enzo slipped inside him, the tickle of the fur on Enzo's chest against his sweaty body so sensual. Coupled with the lightest of kisses on the sweet spot at the back of his neck, it made Shaun putty in Enzo's hands.

Enzo gripped him by the waist and started to really pump him. Enzo favoured long strokes which gave Shaun the maximum pleasure.

"I won't take long," Enzo whispered. "Make yourself come for me."

Obediently, Shaun gripped his aching cock and tugged at it in time to Enzo's plunging in and out of his ass.

Enzo gripped his shoulder with one hand and slapped his arse cheek with the other. "I'm going to come," he announced.

Shaun wasn't far off either. Enzo fucked him faster as he chased his own orgasm. Before long, Enzo grunted and squeezed Shaun's hipbone hard.

Then Shaun came as though his whole body was under Enzo's control. The sensation flooded every nerve ending. Enzo was still filling him, making his orgasm all the more powerful. Shaun had to bury his face in the pillow for fear of screaming the house down.

Once both their breathing had returned to normal, Enzo pulled out of Shaun and disposed of the condom. Shaun rolled onto his back and reached out for Enzo's perspiring body. He didn't care that they were covered in sweat, or that he'd left a wet patch on the bed. He craved that skin-on-skin contact again. Enzo seemed happy to oblige and rested his head on Shaun's chest while Shaun stroked his thick dark hair.

"You are incredible," Enzo whispered.

They lay like that, in silence. It took Enzo's soft snores to make Shaun realise he'd fallen asleep. Carefully, without disturbing him he managed to wrap them both in the duvet.

The movement caused Enzo to roll off him and settle on the pillow. Watching him sleep, Shaun knew that this was more than just two people clinging together in an impossible situation. The man sleeping next to him was rapidly becoming so important to him that it scared him.

He wanted to feel the happiness that should come with a new affair. But as he looked at the hard muscular body he'd been enjoying only minutes earlier, he thought about what he would have done if someone had put a bullet in it today. It didn't bear thinking about.

It didn't happen though, he tried to reason. The fear on Dolly's face when she'd heard Giovanni had been hit told him she was in as deep as he was. She had been so strong and practical, but even Dolly had her limits.

Could he handle being the partner of a gangster? With doubts coursing through his mind, he lay with his back to Enzo, once again out of control and afraid.

Chapter Seventeen

"I need you to move some stock," Marco said to Enzo. "The sellers in the Northern Quarter are getting edgy. They want to know we've more where that came from if they are to turn their backs on Jonny. So, I need you to give them a bit of a show. Let them know we can deliver."

They sat around the kitchen table, Shaun clearing away the breakfast things. He wished they would take this kind of talk into the lounge or the office. The less he knew the better.

"Sure thing," Enzo said.

"You'll have to go on your own though," Marco continued. "If Liam or I set foot out of here, Wellingham will probably have a bullet for us."

"And what about Enzo?" Shaun asked.

"Sorry?" Marco said, seeming totally confused by this new-found interest of Shaun's in their operations.

Shaun realised he was probably speaking out of turn, but his fears from the night before hadn't left him.

He couldn't help himself. "What will happen to Enzo if Jonny catches him, or does that not matter?"

"Of course it matters," Marco replied. "But he's less likely to finish him in cold blood. He would probably take him for leverage."

Shaun threw a tea towel down. "Oh well, that's all right then."

"Shaun—" Enzo started.

But he didn't wait for the reply and stormed outside into the cold winter's day. The farmhouse had got way too claustrophobic for him. He had thought that he and Enzo giving in to their feelings would make his time there easier, but instead it had laid a whole new layer of complications on things.

How did Liam stand it? Usually, he was glued to Marco like a limpet but when he wasn't, how did he not drive himself crazy with worry?

Shaun walked over to the wall and stared down the valley. Things were so peaceful out here compared to the endless drama going on inside those four walls. A few sheep were in the fields, like little clouds had come down to earth. Shaun watched them nibbling away.

He was glad they had the farm. It gave them a sanctuary and breathing space. But for how long? Jonny seemed to be moving closer every chance he got.

The kitchen door creaked open. Shaun turned to see Enzo coming towards him. He looked so handsome that Shaun's heart ached about the situation they were trapped in.

"Shaun. You need to be more careful than that," Enzo said, taking hold of Shaun's arms. "Marco is asking all sorts of questions."

"It's not me that has to be careful," Shaun replied. "I can't help it. I don't like you going on your own. It terrifies me."

Glancing at the house, Enzo stroked Shaun's cheek. "I will be fine. I'm a big boy, remember?"

"Oh, I remember," Shaun said with a smile that he didn't really mean.

Enzo rattled the car keys. "I will be home before you know it."

Shaun followed him around the side of the barn to where the cars were kept. They were out of sight of the house now. Shaun drew him close and luxuriated in the smell of him. The heat from him stopped the chills. Shaun hadn't thought to wrap up when he'd made yet another dramatic exit.

Lifting his head, he didn't even try to stop the tears even though the freezing December day made them feel like shards of ice on his face.

"Hey now," Enzo said, kissing him.

"Come back as soon as you can," Shaun pleaded.

Enzo stroked his hair. "I will. Then you can show me tonight how pleased you are to see me. Do we have a deal?"

Shaun nodded. "We have a deal."

Reluctantly, Shaun let Enzo break from him and get in the car. He stood by the wall of the barn and watched him drive down the track. God, he hated this so bloody much. But the only way to get through the next few hours would be to stay busy.

Wiping his eyes, he returned to the house. It was the last place on earth he wanted to be right then, but what choice did he have? He'd finish cleaning up, then have a look at the camera kit from Dolly.

In the kitchen, everyone had made themselves scarce so he carried on loading the dishwasher. He could still smell Enzo on his clothes. He drank it in.

"Are you okay?" Claire asked, as she came in from the lounge.

Shaun shook his head.

"Want to talk?" she ventured. She sat at the table and picked at the grapes in the bowl.

Sighing, he stopped and sat opposite her. "You know, don't you?"

Claire nodded. "I caught Enzo buying condoms in the supermarket. I didn't have to be Miss Marple to work out the rest. Dolly's a wild one but I think even she would draw the line at taking on two brothers at the same time. Actually, she probably wouldn't, but let's not go there."

It had been foolish to think they could keep a secret in this house. That meant it was only a matter of time until Marco found out. He probably already suspected after Shaun's outburst moments before.

"You bagged yourself a stunner though," Claire said, leaning over and squeezing his hand.

Shaun met her gaze. "For how long, eh? Giovanni could have been killed yesterday. Liam could have been killed months ago. Is today Enzo's turn, or tomorrow? Am I expected to just sit here and wait?"

It felt good to get his words out. If he'd learnt one thing recently, a problem shared was a problem halved. But it could only do so much. Talking wasn't going to fix this bloody war.

Claire exhaled, uncomfortable.

"You don't have to answer that," he said. "The fact is that yes, I am."

"Shaun…"

But he'd had enough of baring his soul for the day. He needed solitude to get through this. Meditation would see him through it.

"I've got some reading to do," he said. "Can you finish up in here?"

"Of course," Claire replied.

He went upstairs and almost bumped into Dolly coming out of the bathroom. She looked exhausted. To his amazement her face was totally devoid of makeup. He had never seen her like that before. She was naturally a very beautiful woman. He wondered if it was the scars inside that she covered with the make-up.

"Oh hello, love," she said, smoothing her hair.

"How's Giovanni?"

"He'll be right as rain in time," she said. "Grumbling like mad about being stuck in bed of course."

"You didn't get much sleep though?" Shaun said.

"I look that bad, do I?" she replied with a sad little laugh.

He didn't dare respond to that. She might be at a low ebb, but she was still Dolly. Instead, he gave her a hug. He hoped to be as big a support to her as she had been to him.

"Thanks, love," she said. "I don't know, eh? What a life we've chosen for ourselves. A little sliver of excitement and a whole wedge of worry. Why do we always go for the bad boys?" She gave him one last sad smile and went into her room, closing the door softly.

Shaun carried on to his room. The sheets were still messed up and he could smell Enzo on them. God, he wanted him in his arms again. He tried not to think about what he was doing right that minute. Down that road lay madness.

He straightened the bed and sat cross-legged. Closing his eyes, he tried to clear his mind the way he had learnt all those years ago. But each time he almost managed it, a snapshot of Enzo would appear, and anxiety would course through his system again.

He tried a few times before giving it up as a bad job. He wasn't a bloody Jedi. Instead, he got his laptop out and started to put together a list of everything he would need at the yoga retreat. This wonderful uncle hadn't given it the green light yet, but it wouldn't hurt to be prepared. He still wouldn't be surprised if this uncle turned out to be a lie. Or worse, a phoney like the Wizard of Oz. Shaun liked to see things in front of him, not suggestions of a saviour.

About an hour into it and he'd barely put anything down. His mind kept wandering. A soft knock on the door disturbed his thoughts. Even though he knew Enzo to be way heavier-handed than that, his heart still wished it was him. "Come in," he ventured, genuinely curious to see who was on the other side.

Liam came through the door. "Hey."

He came in and perched on the end of the bed. He had that nervous face that meant he had something uncomfortable to deal with. Once more Shaun saw a little boy in pyjamas, begging to sleep with him because his nightmares had got the better of him.

"You okay?" Shaun asked, patting the bed.

"Marco said you were a bit upset before," Liam said carefully as he sat.

Shaun sighed. He was getting sick of every move he made being analysed and picked over. "And sent you to come and straighten me out?"

"It's not like that," Liam continued. "He's worried about you."

"No, he fucking isn't," Shaun raged. "All he cares about is that Enzo makes the drop, and the money keeps rolling in. Then tomorrow there might be some girls need dealing with so Enzo and Claire will be expected to put their safety at risk. Then what? You? Me?"

"When Uncle—"

Shaun slammed the lid down on the laptop. "Don't give me the 'when Uncle Z comes' story again. Where is he on his white charger? We don't even know he exists, for Christ's sake."

Liam waited until he finished. He always did that and it riled Shaun all the more. As the big brother, he should be the calm one, but Liam role-reversed things every single time.

"That was the other reason I came," he said calmly. "He's been in touch. They're coming soon. I mean this side of Christmas."

The anger in Shaun paused at this news. "What?"

Liam hugged his knees. He always used to do that when he was anxious, an occurrence that happened far too often. "If Jonny has more men, they want to match him," he explained. "They're going to finish training the men up here. They're going to strike Wellingham big-time."

Shaun shivered. "What does that mean?"

"All-out war."

Chapter Eighteen

He threw the last of the things in his bag and zipped it up. His heart was going ten to the dozen, but this time he wouldn't be swayed. As soon as Liam had gone, Shaun had made the decision and got moving. Only fear could drive a man to move so quickly and Shaun had it in bucketloads.

Passport.

As he got it from the nightstand drawer, the door opened. Once more, Enzo stood in the doorway. Indecision crept into Shaun's head, but he couldn't allow it. His focus had to be on safety.

"Hi. I thought I would tell you I am home," Enzo said. His gaze drawn to the bag on the bed, he came in and shut the door behind him.

Shaun was dreading this talk. It was inevitable and he'd rehearsed what he would say, but now that the man he cared deeply for stood in front of him, he wavered. "Enzo—"

"What is going on here?"

Shaun shoved the passport in his rucksack. He knew what he had to do. He had been a misfit all his life and at this farmhouse was no exception. Enzo had made him feel a sense of belonging, but what good would that be if they both ended up riddled with bullets?

"Are you running out on me?" Enzo asked.

Shaun fought the tears. The hurt on Enzo's face was too much to bear. They had found happiness and under any other circumstances, wild horses wouldn't drag Shaun away. But the last few months had been unbearable. They would be nothing compared to an all-out war.

"Come with me?" he managed. Enzo would never leave. But if Shaun didn't try, he would always wonder what if.

Enzo sat on the bed and ran his hands through his hair. "I can't leave them like this. Giovanni can hardly move. What about your brother?"

Guilt stabbed him straight in the heart. He was running out on Liam again, just like when he'd been a teenager. But the fear of what would happen if he stayed here was overwhelming. He had to keep it together. Marco was Liam's future, not Shaun.

"I can't be responsible for his choices," he said. "Your bloody Uncle Z is planning a war when he gets here. I'm not cut out for this. I can't take it."

Enzo leapt off the bed and took hold of him. Shaun had once revelled in those strong arms, but now he felt controlled and trapped.

"You were just going to leave?" Enzo snarled. "Not even a fucking note?"

Shaun shook himself free and moved over to the window. "No, of course not. I was waiting for you. But since you're doing your ridiculous family honour shit,

I'll be going. When it's over, if you make it, give me a call."

Enzo stood there, his fists balled. Shaun desperately wanted to go over and say he wouldn't go, let him undress him and make the world go away for a while. But it would come back the minute they were apart. The fear every time Enzo left the farm, or never being able to even go to the shops. If Jonny dug in, this could go on for years. Jonny Wellingham wouldn't give in easily. Blood would be spilt on both sides, and rivers of it.

"I've done three months of this," Shaun continued. "I can't give my life. I won't. But I mean what I say. I'll wait for you."

"What will you do?" Enzo asked quietly.

"I'll go abroad," Shaun replied. "Once I'm out of the Manchester area, no one will be looking for me. Jonny Wellingham isn't global."

It was like some ridiculous stand-off. Enzo blocked his way to the door and Shaun's heart was telling him to stay. But Shaun had always been ruled by his head. He'd had to be, with a mother like his. He had no idea where he would go. He had friends in the South of France. He'd start there and see where the wind took him.

He meant what he said. If Enzo made it, perhaps there would be a chance for them later down the line. Or maybe he just wanted to convince himself of that to make leaving easier.

"Please, Enzo," Shaun said. "Let me go."

A tear escaped Enzo's eye. He didn't move to wipe it away. "We love each other," he said.

Shaun had suspected Enzo would push him to this point. He'd rehearsed this line a thousand times that afternoon in the hope that he wouldn't have to use it.

"I don't love you," Shaun said. "You were just a distraction while I was here. Like Dolly and Giovanni. They won't last five minutes when we're free of this crap. And you know what? Neither would we. A clean break is probably better."

He might as well have stabbed Enzo in the heart. The colour drained from him, and he bowed his head. "I don't believe you," he said quietly.

This was becoming one of the hardest things he had ever done. To hurt the man he loved.

"It's true. I'm a selfish bastard, Enzo. I don't do commitment. Ask Liam," he said. "I abandoned him as a kid and now I'm doing it again. Do you think I can't do the same to you or anyone else? You have to think about number one in this life. A lesson you could fucking learn."

Slowly and wordlessly, Enzo moved out of the way, clearing Shaun's path to the door.

The tears were threatening to get out of control now, so Shaun just grabbed the bag and rucksack and fled. He dashed straight down the stairs and out into the cold December night. Thankfully the kitchen was deserted so no one else could try and stop him. If he'd bumped into Liam, his resolve might not have held.

Fighting the urge to throw up, he marched down the path. The tears were rolling down his cheeks, but he didn't dare wipe them because there would be a figure in an upstairs window in the farmhouse watching his every move.

He couldn't show doubt. Instead, he put one foot in front of the other and made his way toward freedom.

* * * *

He'd been in the bus shelter for half an hour, but it had felt like a day. True to form, the rainclouds had opened up about halfway down the farm track. Just as he came around the corner, the bus had driven off down the road. Typical it would be on time just when Shaun didn't need it to be. As the village was miles away from anywhere, they only had one bus an hour.

So, Shaun found himself sitting in cold damp clothes under a harsh light in the centre of the village.

It would be just my luck for Becky to turn up.

"You're a fucking liar."

Shaun looked up to see Enzo in front of him. He was soaked in an old fleece, water from his curls dripping down his face.

Now Shaun had to worry about his brain versus his heart versus his cock. "Enzo…come on," he said wearily. "Don't do this."

Enzo sat next to him in the shelter, shivering against the cold. "I don't believe that you're not in love with me."

"Hm, well, I'm running out on you. I think that should be a red flag."

To his horror, Enzo took hold of his hand. The familiar electricity ricocheted through his system and instinctively he tried to pull his hand away, but Enzo held him firm.

"You're scared," he said, leaning close to him. "I understand. I am scared too. We can't just leave them though."

Shaun knew he was right, but the fear paralysed him. He wanted it all to go away.

"You love me," Enzo stated again.

"I would be pretty stupid to fall in love with someone who could be killed at any moment," Shaun fired back.

"What if—"

But Enzo's words were cut short as three SUVs with blacked-out windows roared through the village.

Enzo leapt off the seat and onto the pavement. "What the fuck?"

But Shaun was ahead of him. He already had his phone out and dialled Liam.

"Shaun?" Liam answered. "Aren't you upstairs?"

"Shut up and listen. Wellingham is on his way to you now. Three SUVs. Get out of there."

Liam didn't even respond but terminated the call.

"We have to go," Shaun said to Enzo. "Are you armed?"

Enzo shook his head.

"Fuck. No matter, we have to be there," Shaun said.

They set off running towards the farm track at the edge of the village, Shaun's abandoned suitcase and rucksack the only testament that they had ever been there. As they ran through the village and onto the road, Shaun couldn't bear to think of what was happening up at the farm. They veered onto the track, but it was a winding one up a hill and they wouldn't be able to keep up the pace.

He grabbed Enzo's arm. "Go slower. We can't burn out," he panted.

Enzo nodded and they walked as fast as they could up the hill. It felt maddeningly slow, but Shaun had trained for the Blackpool 10k and knew that stamina would win.

About halfway up the track, they stopped still. Shaun shivered. The skin at the back of his neck prickled and he could imagine people watching them from behind every tree.

"What is it?" Shaun whispered.

"There's no sound," Enzo replied. "I don't like it."

Shots rang out into the night air.

One, two, three, four.

Shaun cried out at every one.

"Enzo. No," he yelled.

Enzo grabbed hold of him and pulled him close.

"We're too late," Shaun sobbed into his chest. "No."

Chapter Nineteen

They stood there, the rain falling on them. Shaun was sobbing so hard he couldn't even register it. Then Enzo tensed. Shaun followed his stare. There were headlights coming over the brow of the hill.

"I'll fucking kill them," Enzo roared, lurching forward.

"No," Shaun said, pulling at his jacket. "They're armed and there's probably loads of them. They'll kill you."

The lead car was getting closer now.

"You can't stop me," Enzo said, writhing himself free. "I will rip them to fucking pieces."

"Like fuck I can't," Shaun replied.

He shoved Enzo hard in the chest and sent him tumbling down into the wood below. It wasn't a big drop, but enough to stun him for the seconds it took for Shaun to jump down and straddle him. Wet leaves and mud soaking through his trousers, he gripped Enzo's body as hard as humanly possible.

"Get off me, Shaun," Enzo snarled, thrashing beneath him.

"We need to find out what's happened up there. Think," Shaun shouted.

The cars were getting closer and Enzo's powerful body beneath Shaun threatened to shove him right off. But he held firm, clutching at Enzo's arms and gritting his teeth. This man would not die on his watch. Absolutely not.

But Enzo had other ideas and wrenched his arms free. He grabbed Shaun by the coat, ready to fling him to the side.

Shaun didn't know what to do, so he kissed him. At first Enzo continued to struggle but then, to his relief, returned the kiss. It wasn't sexual. It was essential. Whatever they would discover, he had to know that he and Enzo were on the same page. Watching Enzo fight a battle he could never win would be too much to bear.

The cars were going past now. Shaun flattened his body against Enzo's and his heart leapt with joy when those strong arms encircled him. The chaos in Enzo seemed to have passed, at least for the time being. This could be the most important kiss of their lives.

Once the cars were gone, the coast seemed clear. He started to move, but Enzo stayed him.

"I'm scared," Enzo said quietly.

His eyes shone in the moonlight and Shaun could see what he must have looked like when he was a little boy. The murderous thug of moments ago had gone.

"Me too," Shaun replied.

But putting it off wasn't going to make it go away. Shaun got to his feet and helped Enzo up. They scrambled onto the road and set off running up the track.

His body was screaming by the time they got to the top. He ignored its pleas and ran into the farmyard. He had to know. No matter what waited for them.

All the lights were on in the farmhouse when they got there. The front door hung off its hinges. Shaun went to go in, but Enzo grabbed him.

"Wait," Enzo urged. "They could have left men as an ambush."

He hadn't even thought of that. It would be the kind of shit trick Wellingham would pull. Glancing at every window for movement, he wished Liam's face would appear there. All he wanted to hear was his brother telling him he'd been paranoid all along.

"What do we do?" he whispered.

Their sanctuary had been breached and the numbness of the fear was the only thing he could sense. He had to know the outcome of this, whether it was good or bad. The uncertainty had become too much to bear.

"The bunker first," Enzo said, nodding towards the barn. "You never know."

Shaun had completely forgotten about the bunker. They dashed across the farmyard to the barn. It was too much to hope for, but the moments seemed to pass in years instead of seconds.

At the hatch, straw had been disturbed. Shaun's heart hammered as Enzo hauled the trapdoor open.

A terrified Liam, Claire and Marco stared back. Marco had a gun trained on them which he lowered when he realised who it was.

To see the face of his brother was almost too much for Shaun to take in. He dropped to his knees and practically pulled Liam out of the hole, flinging his arms around him.

"Oh, thank everything in the world," Shaun exclaimed. "I thought I'd lost you."

They broke apart so Shaun could look at him. He drank in his face. His handsome, wonderful brother was in his arms. He had never been so thankful for anything in his whole life.

"Where's Giovanni and Dolly?" Enzo asked.

Shaun whirled round. In his excitement at seeing Liam, he hadn't even noticed the faces that were missing. Unease ran over him.

Claire went over to Enzo, holding his hands. "She wouldn't leave him," she said. Tears were streaming down her face.

"What do you mean?" Enzo said. "Where the fuck are they?"

Shaun broke free from Liam and ran to his side.

"Giovanni couldn't move quickly enough, Enzo," Marco said, putting his arm around Liam. "We tried but it wasn't possible."

"Wasn't possible?" Enzo shouted.

He looked to the farmhouse. They had to go inside. Shaun would have had to if Liam had been the one in there. He took hold of Enzo's hand. "Together. Yeah?" he said.

An ashen Enzo nodded.

If the gunmen had left an ambush, Shaun didn't fancy their chances. Enzo would rip them limb from limb before he let them stop him finding out what had happened to his brother.

The inside of the house had been ransacked. The kitchen table had been split in two and the Christmas decorations trampled into thousands of pieces. They had done a number on the place. One thing Wellingham's Boys were good at was wreaking havoc.

Upstairs, more of the same greeted them. Every door lay wide open, as if proud of the destruction that had gone on in there. All except for one door.

The door to Dolly's bedroom remained closed. Shaun glanced at Enzo. He returned the stare. That fearful little boy stared back at him. Shaun brought his hand up and kissed it.

"Come on," he said.

Enzo reached forward and turned the handle. He pushed the door open, and Shaun cried out.

Dolly lay slumped over the lifeless body of Giovanni. Both had been shot at point blank range.

The cry of rage and sorrow that emerged from Enzo would haunt Shaun for the rest of his days. He dropped to his knees and Shaun fell to his side, wrapping his arms around him.

"Oh no," Claire cried as she ran down the landing. "No. No. No." She ran to Dolly, buried her face in her friend's hair and sobbed. But Shaun could see there was nothing they could do for her now.

The energy radiating from Enzo terrified Shaun. He had never seen someone so possessed. His eyes were wild and didn't even seem to register the others.

Then Enzo stood up, brushing Shaun away. Liam and Marco were in the doorway, looking aghast the scene before them. Liam ran to Claire and tried his best to comfort her.

"Give me that gun," Enzo said to Marco.

"What?" Shaun cried, scrambling to his feet. "No."

He ran in between the two, but Enzo put his hand out to Marco. "Give it to me, Marco."

Marco nodded slowly and handed over the firearm.

"You fucking idiot," Shaun screamed in his face. "Why would you do that?"

Enzo pushed past them all and walked towards the staircase. But Shaun couldn't let this happen. He ran after him, grasping at his shoulder. But he might as well have been a fly trying to stop a racehorse.

"Enzo. Don't do this," he pleaded.

But Enzo wouldn't listen. He made it to the top of the stairs, his hand on the banister. Shaun felt time slipping away.

"Stay and listen to me, you fucking coward," Shaun screamed.

Enzo stopped and slowly turned around. "What did you just call me?"

Shaun dropped to his knees. He grabbed hold of Enzo's trousers, then gripped onto his legs.

"Please don't leave me, Enzo," Shaun cried. "If you shoot them, they'll lock you up and throw away the key. I'm begging you not to."

Enzo looked down at him. "But you'd be fucking stupid to fall in love with a man like me. Weren't they your words?"

He wrenched himself free of Shaun's grasp and backed off.

"Look at me now," he said. "I've got nothing. No brother. No lover. Why should I care?"

Shaun leapt to his feet, gripping onto Enzo's jacket. "Because you have a lover. Because I bloody love you."

His tears were flowing freely, and he felt sure snot would be running down his face, but he didn't care. Shaun would have walked over hot coals at that point to stop Enzo from throwing his life away. *Their* life away.

"Don't leave me," Shaun sobbed. "I'm begging you. I need you."

Enzo bowed his head. "I won't go," he said quietly.

Shaun flung his arms around those broad shoulders that hung limply. He made a vow to himself then and there that he would never let go of this man again. He would force life back into him if that was what it took.

Chapter Twenty

They lay entwined in each other's arms as the dawn light broke through the curtains they'd left open. Neither of them had expected to get any sleep that night, but once the tears had all been cried, they were both spent and fell asleep around five.

Shaun squinted as the strong winter sun burst in, bathing the bed in warm light. The storm of the night before had passed.

"What time is it?" Enzo said quietly.

"Just after eight," Shaun replied, glancing at the clock.

He lay on the pillow, the events of the last twenty-four hours replaying in his mind at warp speed. How could it have happened?

"How are you feeling?" he asked, turning to face Enzo. He reached out and squeezed his arm, then took his hand and held it.

"I feel topsy-turvy," Enzo said.

Shaun kissed his knuckles. Enzo could be so childlike sometimes it made Shaun want to protect him at all costs. "In what way?" he asked softly. "Talk to me."

"I am devastated that Giovanni is gone," Enzo said, his eyes filling with fresh tears. "I can't believe it. Ever since we were kids, he has been everything to me. What am I going to do? How do I tell Mama?"

Shaun had no power to make this better, no matter how much he wished it. If it had been Liam instead of Giovanni, he would have been inconsolable. He still felt bad for his elation when he'd dragged Liam out of that bunker. He hadn't even stopped to do a head count, the relief had been so great.

"We will figure it out together," Shaun whispered. "You have me now."

"That is why I feel so mixed up inside," Enzo replied. "To have you here in my arms. Properly, not sneaking around. It feels incredible. But my brother is lying dead just feet from here. I can't even tell him that I love you."

Enzo burst into tears, wracking sobs that came from his very core. The pain Shaun experienced watching him go through this made him want to rip Jonny Wellingham limb from limb.

Instead, he scooted forward and kissed him. "And that is natural and fine. Don't go beating yourself up about your feelings. I don't. I act on them all the time. In case you hadn't noticed."

Enzo smiled through his tears. "And that is something we're going to have to talk about. If this is going to become a thing."

Shaun rolled his eyes. "This is already a thing, knobhead."

Enzo kissed him. He stroked Shaun's hipbone and ran his hand lightly around to his arse cheek.

"I know I said that I wouldn't do anything to risk us..."

Shaun frowned. He didn't like the sound of this. "Yes?"

"I meant what I said," Enzo replied. "You stopped me doing something stupid last night and I will be forever grateful. I will make sure we get our revenge on him, but this has to be done carefully."

The real world was banging on the door again and Shaun felt ill at the thought of what the next twist would be in this horrific situation. But he couldn't bear to think about it right now. All he wanted was Enzo.

He snuggled into his arms and kissed him. A long, slow kiss that Shaun never wanted to end. He stroked Enzo's furry chest and luxuriated in the heat from his body. Enzo rolled onto his back and Shaun crawled on top of him. Enzo wrapped his legs around Shaun, and they carried on kissing.

In between tears and anger last night, there had been no time for sex. But now Shaun needed that closeness to Enzo and the way that Enzo responded, he needed it too.

Enzo gripped Shaun's shoulders and squeezed him close. It was as though they were melding themselves into one person.

Shaun sat up so he knelt above Enzo, then threw the duvet off them. The cold air of the winter morning didn't register as their bodies heated up for each other. Stroking Enzo's body, Shaun took hold of his solid cock. He rubbed his thumb over the head. Enzo sighed.

"Your touch is perfect," he said.

His mission was to give Enzo some respite from the emotions that were swirling around inside him. Shaun leant down and took his cock in his mouth.

Enzo moaned and closed his eyes. Shaun sucked lightly. He didn't want Enzo to feel the emotions of a quick fuck, but instead those of making love. Holding Enzo's cock steady, Shaun licked his balls. Enzo quivered as Shaun applied the lightest pressure.

He massaged Enzo's cock and sucked at his balls. Enzo gripped the pillows as he let Shaun take control.

"I need you," Enzo whispered.

Shaun took the hint and reached across to the nightstand where the condoms and lube were. Enzo tried to move but Shaun shook his head.

"Let me," he said. Expertly rolling the condom onto Enzo's cock, he liberally applied the lube to his own hole.

"Are you sure you're ready?" Enzo asked.

"Where you're concerned, I was born ready," Shaun replied. He punctuated the statement with another long, slow kiss. Fuck—if he spent the rest of his days kissing this man, he would die happy.

Then he positioned himself so he sat on top of Enzo's big dick. It was true, he usually liked to be prepared for such an invasion, but this morning his need was as great as his lover's. Only sex could bring this disconnection from the world.

Enzo's cock breached him. Shaun revelled in the feelings that swept through his body. They maintained eye contact as Shaun slid down the length of him. Enzo took hold of Shaun's hands, entwining their fingers. Shaun took them and ran them over his body. A tear ran down Enzo's cheek.

"Shaun..."

"I know," Shaun replied, leaning down and licking the tear away.

They were still for a second. Shaun trusted this man and the look in Enzo's eyes told him the feeling was mutual. They had been through so much together that a bond had formed that both scared and exhilarated Shaun. He supposed that was true love.

Totally in sync, they moved their hips slowly. Shaun felt so close to Enzo right now. He wanted to take all the pain away. Not forever—he didn't have the strength for that. But they could both live in this moment.

He kept the rhythm, not too fast and not too slow. Stretching, he let Enzo run his hands freely over his body. Enzo gripped Shaun's cock and tugged it in time with their hips.

"Fuck, you are so perfect," Enzo murmured.

They both knew that wasn't true, but Shaun was fast falling in love with Enzo and he liked seeing himself through his eyes.

"Come for me," Shaun said.

"Make me," Enzo replied.

Shaun nodded and they fucked harder. He held on to the headboard as he rode Enzo. He didn't care if the bed made a noise. They needed this and woe betide anyone who complained.

He bucked his hips faster, staring down at the incredibly handsome and wounded man beneath him. He ran his hands over Enzo's cheek and traced his lips. Enzo licked at his finger, biting the tip.

"I'm close," Enzo said.

Shaun leant back, supporting himself on Enzo's thick, muscular thighs. He rode his cock harder. Enzo thrashed on the pillow.

"Oh God, yeah," he cried.

Then his body dissolved into spasms, and he gripped Shaun's waist hard. Shaun continued to work his dick, wanting to squeeze every last drop out of him. His cries rang out but he didn't care. They were a sign of life and love, something the house needed.

When Enzo opened his eyes, Shaun climbed off and lay next to him. Even though it was cold, they were both covered in sweat.

Enzo turned onto his side and took hold of Shaun's cock.

"It doesn't matter about me," Shaun whispered, stroking Enzo's cheek.

"My love. It always matters about you," Enzo replied, kissing him. He tugged hard at Shaun's cock. "Relax into it," he whispered into Shaun's ear.

Shaun did so and, with his free hand, Enzo grabbed him by the back of the head and pulled him up for a kiss.

It didn't take long until the release came, and Shaun groaned into Enzo's mouth. Panting, they kissed hard as the orgasm ripped through Shaun's body, his whole frame tense as Enzo took him over the edge.

His cum covered his body as he rode the wave of pleasure.

Enzo carefully rested his head back on the pillow and retrieved the towel they had thrown on the chair in the corner. Gently and methodically, he cleaned Shaun's body. All the while, he never once broke eye contact.

Then he threw the towel in the corner and took Shaun in his arms. If the events of the night before hadn't left them absolutely bereft, it would have been the most romantic moment in Shaun's life.

"Can I ask you something?" Shaun said when they broke the kiss.

"Of course," Enzo said, stroking his hair.

"Last night. At the bus stop," he began. "You started saying what if. Then those bastards went past. What did you mean?"

Enzo rolled onto his back. Shaun felt the absence of his touch keenly and sat up.

"Please tell me," he said, running his hand across Enzo's furry chest.

"I won't lie to you, Shaun," Enzo said, staring up at the ceiling. "I was going to say what if I gave all this up?"

The words that Shaun had hoped to hear over anything else were tumbling from Enzo's lips. "And now?" he asked, not even bothering to keep the hopeful tone out of his voice.

"Now? I want that bastard's head for what he's done to my family. I would not be honouring the memory of my father if I let this go unpunished. I want to take his blood to Mama and show her he suffered."

Shaun felt as though he'd climbed all the way out of a huge hole only to tumble backwards into the darkness again.

"Enzo!" Marco shouted from the landing.

"Oh, what the fuck now?" Shaun wailed.

"Come on," Enzo said. He sprang out of the bed and grabbed a towel. Shaun followed him, putting on his bathrobe. Once more, adrenaline pumped through his veins. After last night, he'd doubted if his body could even produce any more but…

Out on the landing, a silent Claire and a wide-eyed Liam were waiting for them. Shaun hated to see fear on his brother's face again. He went to his side and grabbed hold of his hand.

"There's five SUVs coming down the track," Marco said. "We haven't got time for the bunker."

He thrust a gun into Enzo's hand, and they all ran down the stairs. They couldn't be here, could they? Would Wellingham finish them off in broad daylight? Of course he would.

"You three. Stay behind us and if you get a chance to break for the bunker, take it," Marco shouted. "Or better still the woods. Just run and don't look back."

Liam and Shaun glanced at each other. They both knew they wouldn't do that. If there was to be a fight, it would be all of them.

Shaun's heart was pounding out of his chest as they ran through the broken front door. He grabbed a piece of wood that had nails still in the end. Liam, following his lead, picked up the heavy plant pot that Dolly had used for her cigarette butts.

The five SUVs drew up to the farmyard. They had no chance of getting past this lot. Shaun was ready to meet his fate with the two men he loved most in the world. But they wouldn't take him without a fight and if he could slam these nails into Wellingham's face, then all the better.

With his free hand, he reached for Enzo's, squeezing it.

Enzo seemed scared but resolute. Shaun couldn't look at Liam. If he did, it would all be over.

His heart raced as the door of the central SUV opened. But it wasn't Jonny Wellingham who got out. Instead it was a stunningly handsome man with short grey hair and a tan that certainly did not come from Manchester.

"Uncle Z," Marco shouted. He ran forward and embraced his uncle, who patted him on the back.

"Marco," Uncle Z said, holding him tightly.

Marco broke away and just beamed at him. Men in dark suits were spilling out of the other vehicles now. Shaun had never seen so many attractive men in his life. None were a patch on Enzo though.

Marco brought his uncle over to Liam, who put the plant pot down and rubbed his hands on his hoodie.

"Uncle Z, this is Liam. My special someone," Marco announced proudly.

"Ah, Liam," Uncle Z exclaimed. "I have seen so many photos of you from Marco. It is nice to finally meet you in the flesh."

He pulled Liam into a warm embrace. Full of energy, he broke away and turned to Enzo, throwing his arms around him.

"Enzo," he said. "I am so sorry. They will pay. That I can promise you."

Enzo nodded. "Thank you."

Then his gaze fell on Shaun. It was the kind of look that could either send a person to heaven or hell. Shaun felt excited and terrified all in one go.

"And who are you?" he asked. "Armed for battle, I see."

Shaun dropped the wood and stepped forward. "I'm Shaun. Liam's brother and Enzo's…"

Enzo put his arm around him. "My lover."

"I see we have sad and wonderful news," the Italian said, taking Shaun's hand. "I'm pleased to meet you. I'm Lorenzo de Luca."

Chapter Twenty-One

Lorenzo's men had done a good job of clearing the lounge up. The forced family of sorts sat in a circle by the fire.

"Thank you for dealing with everything, Uncle," Marco said.

Lorenzo sat in the armchair, nursing a brandy. "Think nothing of it."

The rest of the house had been filled to the rafters. Once Lorenzo had made his grand entrance, they had leapt into action. His men dealt with Dolly and Giovanni's bodies. They were in the barn, still together. Lorenzo declared they wouldn't be separated again. Enzo had simply nodded and left them to it.

Shaun and Liam had directed this new mob to any spare bit of floor they could find to make beds on. It felt good to be working on something together. Every so often, Shaun would break to find Enzo. He would usually be found talking to one of the new men. They favoured Italian. Shaun suspected they were hatching plots of revenge.

"They're going to kill them all, aren't they?" Shaun said to Liam as they wrestled with yet another duvet.

"I can't see any other end to this," Liam replied grimly.

"There was a time I would have jumped at the chance to be squashed in with all these handsome men. But now…"

Liam stopped. "And now?"

"Now I just want one. I can't lose him, Liam."

Dropping the bed linen, Liam gave him a hug. "No one is losing anyone. Uncle Z is here now. Things will get better. I know it."

Claire was harder to get through to. She hadn't spoken a word since they had found Dolly and Giovanni.

She sat in the far corner of the room. It seemed to be more than she could bear to be alone, but she wasn't yet ready to talk. She pulled her hoodie closer around her and watched them all intently.

"Shock comes in many forms," Lorenzo said to Liam when he tried to offer her some food. "Leave her be. She will come back to us."

Liam settled down in Marco's outstretched arms on the sofa.

"You said it would be a time for stories later," Shaun said. "Is it later now?"

He snuggled up to Enzo on the floor by the fire. It felt nice to be open and honest about what they had going on. He hoped that would be the case for the rest of his life.

The firelight twinkled in Lorenzo's eyes as he leant forward. "I think that is fair. So yes, I am the Lorenzo de Luca that Jonny fucking Wellingham thinks he put in the bottom of the Mersey."

Knowing how totally inappropriate it was, Shaun couldn't fight the grin that appeared on his face. The magnitude of this was huge. He'd thought a new market had been their motivation, but revenge had been on Lorenzo's mind the whole time. Pure and simple. He gave an involuntary shudder.

"Shit," he said. "That is the plot twist that I didn't see coming. This would make an amazing Netflix series. I hope you're taking notes, Liam."

Marco handed him the joint. They had all cheered when he'd got his pot box out. Even Lorenzo had partaken, and one had turned into quite a few.

"How come you're not dead then?" Shaun asked, taking a drag.

"Because Jonny Wellingham couldn't organise a piss-up in a brewery," Lorenzo replied. "Sure, they put a couple of bullets in me. The stupid bastards didn't check where though. Don't get me wrong—it was touch and go there for a while, but I pulled through. Not that I remember much of it."

Shaun couldn't believe it. "And you made your way home to Italy to plot your revenge. It's brilliant. Jonny Wellingham will shit when he realises what's happened. Were you very close? Please don't tell me you were in love with him."

Lorenzo burst out laughing. "Not quite. Give me some credit. Could anyone love that overgrown broom handle? I was only ever over here to wait until my father could get a road in. It never happened. Let's say, Manchester has always been on the back burner. After what happened in Naples—"

He stopped and glanced over at Marco. Enzo wrapped his arms tighter around Shaun, who squeezed him. He had been through so much grief in the last six months. It would be a long road until he healed. But Shaun was willing to travel it with him. Every step of the way. Together.

"We had to rebuild from the ground up," Lorenzo continued. "I figured we could do that just as easily in Manchester and I'd finally do what Papa didn't."

"And settle a score in the meantime," Shaun said, passing him the joint.

"There's always collateral damage," Lorenzo said. "But yes, Jonny Wellingham will be made to pay for what he did years ago and what he did hours ago. Believe me, if he thinks he had trouble before, his life is going to get ten times more difficult now I am here."

The look of anticipation on his face made Shaun's body run cold. This man had done what he needed to for survival.

He settled into Enzo's arms. The initial euphoria of the surprise settled into an overwhelming feeling of dread. The future terrified him.

Liam left the room to get more wine. Shaun slipped from Enzo's arms and followed him.

The kitchen had about six men sat around the patched-up table. They were all drinking beer and had pop music playing. They hastily switched it off when Shaun and Liam entered the room.

"Don't worry about it," Liam said. "You've worked wonders today. You deserve some down time."

He got a couple of bottles from the rack and stopped in his tracks when he saw his brother behind him. "Shaun. What's up?"

"What's up?" Shaun whispered. "Did you hear him in there? He's going to wipe out the whole lot of them."

"What did you expect? Wellingham declared war, not Lorenzo."

Shaun took the bottles from Liam's hands, placing them on the table.

"What are you doing?" Liam asked, confused.

"Outside. Now."

They both went out onto the yard. The wind was whipping up and Shaun pulled his hoodie closer to him.

"It's freezing. Make it quick," Liam said, shivering.

"We have to get out of here," Shaun said. "This is going to turn into the bastard Sopranos. If we're lucky, we'll get a long stretch inside. That's if we're *lucky*, Liam."

Liam flushed. "What is it with you and running out? You're doing it on an hourly basis these days. Surely Enzo is enough to make you stay, even if I'm not."

The moon shone down on them. Shaun couldn't take much more of this emotion. "I want us all to live, Liam. Look at this lot. Who are we sharing a house with? This is out of control."

He started to pace up and down. He always did that when he was stressed.

"Don't start the bloody walking," Liam said. "This has always been Lorenzo's house. The offer of your business was from Lorenzo. Do you expect him to sleep in the barn?"

The reality that he would always be linked to this world hit Shaun like a sledgehammer. But he was too far gone now to be able to do anything about it. That didn't mean he couldn't be safe.

"Liam. We can't help them," Shaun replied. "We don't know this world, not really. Talk to them. We can go away. Maybe Enzo could come with us as bodyguard?"

Liam shook his head. "Yeah. I'll just leave Marco, shall I? As long as you've got your man, eh?"

"I didn't mean it like that. You know I didn't," Shaun pleaded. As usual, his words were coming out all wrong. "You and me then. We can be safe. Marco and Enzo can come to us when this is all over."

Liam shook his head. "I can't go. You wouldn't really leave Enzo. Not now. You'd spend your life worrying. Surely it's better to be here?"

Liam had him there. When Shaun had walked down the farm track the night before, he'd been sure that running was the best option. But when Enzo had arrived at the bus stop, Shaun had realised that he couldn't be without him.

"You're right," he said quietly. "I love him so much. I'm not leaving his side. But this life is too much. You've had ten years to get used to all this fucking drama. I hate it."

Liam nodded and went back to the farm. Shaun watched him go and his heart leapt when he saw Enzo silhouetted in the doorway. He had a way of standing that sent Shaun crazy. He exuded strength and power.

Silently, Enzo came over to Shaun. He'd brought a blanket that he wrapped Shaun in and drew him close. That special musky Enzo smell instantly settled Shaun. It wasn't the times when he was in Enzo's arms that he worried about though. It was the long nights that he would spend worrying whether Enzo would come home.

"You are really that scared?" Enzo said.

"Of course, I am. You should be too," Shaun replied, looking up at him. "Now I've got you, I can't lose you, Enzo. Don't you care that I might be in danger? Think about what we could have without all this shit."

"I have to avenge my brother's death," Enzo said firmly. "I have to."

Shaun gripped hold of his shirt. "Don't you see? Living a full and happy life is the best way to pay tribute to Giovanni. Not getting a life sentence or worse. You and I could do that. We could start the business together. No looking over our shoulders. Just us, living our lives. Think Enzo. Think of the life we'd share. Just us."

Enzo held him closer. Shaun hardly dared to hope that his silence meant he was actually considering it. His whole body shook. He didn't know if it was the cold or the desperation.

"That would be quite the jump," Enzo said eventually. "I was raised for this life. I would have to be certain before I walked away."

"Certain?" Shaun asked incredulously. "What more do you want me to do? I draw the line at any further public humiliation. Begging for your love in front of Marco and my brother is quite enough for anyone."

Enzo smiled. "I strike a hard bargain, don't I?"

"You sure do," Shaun muttered. "What do you want from me, Enzo? Name it and I will do it."

"How about a kiss?"

"A kiss?" Shaun repeated. "That I can do."

They moved closer.

"But you have to make this one really count," Enzo whispered. "If I'm going to change my whole life for you, I need to feel it."

Shaun kissed Enzo like he'd never kissed a man in his life. The pressure and terror of the last few months spilled out of him in passion. He gripped Enzo's hair and dove his tongue into his mouth. He pushed his body against Enzo, wrapping his arms around his shoulders.

Eventually a dazed Enzo broke away. "Jesus Christ. When you put it like that—"

But Shaun hadn't finished. He kissed Enzo again. Running his hands through Enzo's hair, he wanted him to realise just how deeply he had fallen in love.

"Well?" Shaun asked when they separated. "Put me out of my misery."

"Okay," Enzo said. "You win."

* * * *

The car bumped down the farm track and into the village.

"Stop," Shaun said. "I've left that application form in the back."

"You've checked it a thousand times," Enzo grumbled. "It is all correct, Shaun."

"Pretty please."

Enzo sighed and pulled over by the bus stop. Shaun hopped out and started to rifle in the boot. He wanted to make sure everything was right so he could get a new passport as quickly as possible. Typical of him to be running away with a handsome Italian and he'd left his passport at the bus stop.

"Shaun, love. Is that you?"

He stuck his head around the side of the car and saw Jean, Enzo's number-one fan from yoga.

"Oh, hello, Jean," Shaun said. He really didn't need to be chewing the cud with one of the villagers. He wanted to get Enzo as far away as possible before he could change his mind.

"That other one not with you?" she asked.

Shaun suppressed a smile and leant in the car. "Enzo. Could you come out for a minute?"

Muttering, Enzo got out of the car. Jean's face lit up when she saw him.

"Here he is," Jean said, licking her lips.

"There. I hope that's made your morning better," Shaun said. "Is that what you wanted? It's a bit cold to strip him down but take my word for it, it's all impressive."

Jean's eyebrows raised. "Oh, like that, is it?"

"Yes, Jean. It's like that."

She leant forward. "And I don't bloody blame you either," she said with a chuckle. "Anyway, that's not all that I wanted you for. Did you leave two bags in the bus stop last week?"

Shaun thought he might be about to kiss her or provide her with grandchildren or whatever she needed. Hell, he might even loan her Enzo for a night. "Yes," he squeaked.

"You daft bat," she said. "Lucky I go out every morning at six. It keeps me trim." She glanced at Enzo. "I found them sat there like they'd been left by the tooth fairy. I took them in. I had no number for you. I asked Becky, but she said she had nothing to do with you. I thought you two were friendly? She was quite certain about it."

"Well, you've found me now," Shaun said quickly.

"Come on then," she said. "I've got them in the house."

"I'll wait for you here," Enzo said with a shudder.

Shaun followed Jean into her little cottage and his heart soared when he saw his bags just inside the door. "Thank you so much, Jean. This means so much."

He picked them up and went to go but she stayed him with a hand on his arm. "Listen to me, lad. Now I don't know what's going on up there and I don't want to. But you should get far away from it."

Shaun grinned. "That's exactly what I intend to do."

"Well, off you go then," she said.

"One more thing. Your grandson, Frank," Shaun said.

"What of him?" she asked, frowning.

"I hate to have to tell you this, but he's back on the drugs," Shaun told her. "But I know of a really good rehab place. They're pretty cruel, but it's the only way to get through to them. I'll send you the details."

"Oh, I don't know..." Jean said.

"Tough love, Jean. It'll only be for a few months. It's what he deserves."

"I suppose you're right," she said.

He kissed her on the cheek and went out to the car. Gleefully, he threw his bags onto the back seat and jumped into the passenger seat. "Turn this car around," he said to Enzo.

"What?"

"Nothing is stopping us now. Let's just go and pack the rest of our things and leave tonight."

Enzo looked taken aback but then a smile crept over his lips. "Yes. We leave tonight."

He kissed Shaun long and hard. Shaun would never get used to those kisses, but he intended to spend the rest of his life trying. "*Avanti*, my Italian stud. Take me to your homeland and ravish me."

Enzo winked and fired the car up. They did a full U-turn and sped off back to the farm for what he hoped would be the last time.

Chapter Twenty-Two

It could have been a pile of leaves. A canopy of trees sheltered them from view. The birds were singing and the overwhelming sense of peacefulness felt right.

Shaun and Enzo stood, hand in hand and just stared. It was freezing, but Shaun could barely feel it. They had stood there for a while, just looking and allowing themselves to get lost in their thoughts.

"It's like they never existed," Enzo said. "I can't bear it."

Shaun cuddled into him. "We know they did. That's what really matters."

Enzo wiped a tear from his eye. "This is so hard," he said.

"I know, my love," Shaun replied. "When we get there, we'll create a wonderful peaceful garden where people can go to think. We'll name it after them. Your mother can come and we'll tell her how brave they were."

Enzo beamed. "Can we put some spiky plants in there for Giovanni?"

"Of course, and big vibrant, blousy ones for Doll. She'd love that."

They stared into each other's eyes and burst into tears. Grabbing hold of each other, they stood there, letting time be totally insignificant.

When Shaun eventually broke away, he smiled at the big Italian he had every intention of spending the rest of his life with. "I'll leave you be." Shaun stroked his face. "A bit of alone time, yeah?"

Enzo nodded and kissed him. "I love you, Shaun."

"I love you too."

Shaun walked out of the lovely woodland glade that Lorenzo's boys had chosen for Giovanni and Dolly's final resting place. As spots went, it wasn't a bad place to spend eternity, but he would rather have them here. How he longed for Giovanni to have a go at him about something and Dolly to come and hug it better.

Yet another tear escaped his eye as he climbed out of the little glade. It was swept away on the wind. "Bye, Dolly. Bye, Giovanni," he said softly. He went over the brow of the hill and stopped to take in the view. It never got stale. The valley, all green even in the harsh winter weather.

Rubbing his hands together, he walked down the field towards the farm. Now that he could do what he wanted, he found he would actually miss the old place. *Typical Shaun, spend months plotting escapes, then when the cage door opens, he's terrified.*

As he came into the yard, Liam stood in the upstairs window. Shaun waved but Liam just watched him, his face unmoving. Frowning, Shaun made his way inside. Marco and Lorenzo were in the lounge studying a map.

Shaun did not want to know what for. He was out of this now.

"What's up with face ache?" Shaun asked.

"Who?" Marco replied.

"Bloody Liam," Shaun said. "He just gave me a death stare from upstairs."

Marco and Lorenzo looked at each other. Shaun perched on the edge of the sofa, unwinding his scarf.

"He's upset that you're leaving, Shaun," Marco said, standing and wincing as his back clicked. "We all are."

"You aren't, you fibber," Shaun exclaimed. "I've driven you mad since the moment we met."

Marco swatted him over the head. "I've never had a brother before. You've given me a taste. I quite like it. Some of the time, but that's the point, isn't it?"

Shaun squeezed his leg. "I'll be your brother any day. But maybe ask Liam if it's worth it before you start writing cheques you won't want to cash."

Marco laughed. "I'd better go and see if he's all right."

"I'll come with you," Shaun said.

Lorenzo sat up on the chair. "Actually, Shaun, there is something I want to talk to you about. Where is Enzo?"

Shaun suddenly felt ill. Did Lorenzo have a mission for them? He'd thought that they were going to get out of his clutches.

"Don't look so worried," Lorenzo said with a wink. "It's nothing illegal. Jesus, there are trust issues in this family."

A thousand witty retorts passed over Shaun's lips but in the interests of harmony, they were left unspoken. A gargantuan effort for him. Maybe a leopard could change its spots.

Marco left the room, glancing at his uncle. "He's coming in. Do you want him?"

Lorenzo nodded. He reached across and took Shaun's hands. "You can trust me, you know. Things are different now. I will protect your brother as if he were my own son. You have my solemn promise."

Shaun squeezed his hands. "Lorenzo. I truly do appreciate that. But I will level with you. I would give anything for Liam not to be in love with Marco right now. I don't want my brother to need your protection. Can you understand that?"

Letting his hands drop, Lorenzo got up and stood against the fire. "I appreciate your honest words, Shaun. I do understand, but I'm a realist. Wishing has never done any good. Liam is in some danger. We all are. But I have brought good men."

Shaun nodded. There was nothing else to say. Wild horses wouldn't drag Liam from Marco's side. That had been made evident in the last few months.

"What's going on?" Enzo came into the room.

"Shut the door," Lorenzo said. "Come. Sit."

A wary Enzo sat next to Shaun on the sofa, taking hold of his hand. Lorenzo resumed sitting in the chair and beamed across at them.

"Are you going to milk this moment to death?" Shaun laughed nervously.

"I am," Lorenzo said before reaching into his pocket and pulling out a folded envelope that he handed to Shaun. "You can't deny a man a bit of fun."

Shaun's hand trembled as he straightened the envelope out and opened it. A letter was inside with a solicitor's letterhead. He scanned the words.

Sublet agreement.

But the rest was in Italian. He looked up at Lorenzo.

"I will make it quick," he said. "I am getting older and starting to think of an out. That is why I am so hard on Marco and Liam. One day soon, I will give everything to them, or one of your other cousins perhaps. Who knows?"

Enzo huffed. "Not one of those three, I hope. They are not good enough. You know that, Uncle."

Lorenzo waved his hand. "Anyway, listen to me. You would always have been a contender, but I respect that you have made this decision. As we come to the last battle with Wellingham, it pains me that you won't be by my side."

Shaun panicked that this speech was going to be a recruitment drive. Enzo seemed determined to start their new life, but he still ached to avenge Giovanni.

"He will be safe," Shaun interrupted. "Surely that is important."

"Your lover is fiercely protective, Enzo," Lorenzo said. "I have faced many foes in my time, but I know when I am beaten. What I wanted to say is that one day I wish to retire to Tuscany. It is the most beautiful part of the most beautiful country in the world."

Shaun had no idea where this was going. He tried to study Lorenzo's face for a tell of whether this was good news or bad. Then again, Lorenzo's idea of good probably differed greatly from Shaun's.

"I found a villa in the middle of nowhere. The only downside was a neighbouring house encroaching on my space," Lorenzo continued. "But good news. The owner is dead, and the family sold to me. When they found out who I was, they inflated the price, of course. Absolute criminals."

Fighting the urge to giggle, Shaun watched the indignation pass over Lorenzo's face. He really was a fascinating man. Under different circumstances, Shaun could have gone for him. But he shouldn't even be thinking that while sitting next to the man who was his everything.

He took hold of Enzo's hand and squeezed it.

"Sorry," Lorenzo said, holding his hands up. "Cut a long story short, I got the villa and I'm subletting it to you for fifty years. Now you will have to pay me rent. I think a euro a year is a fair price. Don't you?"

Shaun felt as though he'd been winded. He stared open-mouthed at Lorenzo. He knew the family were keen to invest in a legitimate business, but he had never expected anything like this.

With a flourish, Lorenzo switched on the huge plasma TV above the fireplace and a photo of a sprawling terracotta villa filled the screen. It was huge, with a pool, lots of land and a terrace overlooking the vineyards.

"Are you fucking kidding me?" Shaun said.

"Of course not," Lorenzo replied. "I owe you both and I can't think of anyone I trust more to look after my retirement home. You don't mind running the estate too, do you?"

"Mind?" Shaun said. "I could kiss you, Lorenzo de Luca."

Enzo wrapped his arm around him. "There's only one man you kiss," he said, nuzzling the top of his head. "But, Uncle, what can I say? This is such a lot."

Lorenzo got up and so did Enzo and Shaun. He took Enzo by the hand.

"You have paid more than I can ever repay," he said. "Let me do this for you."

Enzo nodded and flung his arms around Lorenzo.

"You like it then?" Marco came into the room with Liam following. His eyes were red.

"Liam?" Shaun said, going over to him.

"I'm okay," Liam said with a sniff. "I'm just really going to miss you."

Shaun pulled him into a hug. "I'm going to miss you too, you daft sod."

Snuggling into his shoulder, Liam gave a last sob before standing back. "We're not even going to have our Christmas."

It had occurred to Shaun that he had another broken promise to add to his tally. "I know that, kiddo, but I have to get him away," he said quietly. "He could change his mind and do something fucking ridiculous."

"I can hear you," Enzo said.

"You're supposed to," Shaun replied.

Liam sniffed. "I understand. I'd do the same."

"Tuscany for Christmas next year. I absolutely promise," Shaun replied, running his hands through Liam's hair.

"You do?" Liam asked hopefully.

"Of course, I do," Shaun replied. "I love you so much. You mean everything to me, you know that?"

Liam held on to him tight. "I love you too."

Shaun didn't even try to fight the tears. When they broke apart, he wiped his eyes. Then he noticed Marco, Lorenzo and Enzo all rubbing their eyes.

Turning to Liam, they burst into fits of laughter.

"You soft bastards," Liam said with a grin.

Shaun felt happy and sad all at once. It was a heady emotion and he wished he could bottle this moment forever. He hoped to God this was the beginning of something and not the ending of his brother. They had parted before but not with the stakes raised like this.

He caught Enzo's eye, who nodded at him. It was time to go. Their new life awaited them.

He grabbed Liam into another hug. "Please take care of yourself, for fuck's sake. I'm going to insist on daily FaceTime."

Liam squirmed away. "Daily?"

"Yes, daily," Shaun said sternly. He narrowed his eyes at Marco. "Twelve noon, every day. Or there will be an issue. I mean it. Don't make me come back here. I have muscle for backup these days."

Marco held his hands up in protest. "Your wish is my command, Shaun. You'll have no argument from me."

Shaun beamed at him. "Now you're getting the hang of this brother thing."

They all made their way through the house. A house that would benefit from two fewer people being in it. Both their bedrooms had already been claimed so they couldn't change their minds now, even if they wanted to.

Shaun gazed up at Enzo as they walked to the car. He would never ever want to do that. This was the right thing. He was taking his love to safety.

Everyone came out into the yard. That was when Shaun saw Claire stood at the side. She still hadn't spoken and spent most of her time in her room. "One second," he said to Enzo.

He dashed over to her and held her hands. She held his gaze but still couldn't bring herself to speak. It didn't matter to Shaun. There was still someone in there.

"Come back to us, Claire," he said. "Then come to us. Whenever you like. Just come. There will always be a welcome for you. I promise you."

Claire slowly nodded.

He hugged her hard and she returned it, which made his heart dance with joy. With one last look into her eyes, he went back to the car where Enzo waited. "Bye, everyone," he said. "Please, all of you, stay safe."

The tears were flowing freely now, as he got in the car. This was emotion overload and he needed it to be over.

Enzo got in and fired up the engine. They were driving to Tuscany. Liam would send their stuff by courier, but Enzo wouldn't have his sports car shipped, so here they were. Like a modern-day Thelma and Louise but hopefully without the Grand Canyon.

"Drive, hot stuff," Shaun said, grinning at him. "Did I tell you that I love you?"

"Tell me again," Enzo replied.

"I love you."

"I love you too."

Leaning down, Enzo kissed him, long and hard, then dropped the car into gear. With a *vroom*, they set off out of the farmyard and down the track towards the future.

A future Shaun was ready to embrace with open arms.

Want to see more from this author? Here's a taster for you to enjoy!

Two Tribes: Don't Look Back in Anger

Kristian Parker

Excerpt

Lorenzo de Luca turned off the motorway into the suburbs of South Manchester. Back in the day, he'd had a little bedsit around here. It had been fifteen years since he'd been here. Surely they hadn't changed the roads, though.

A building that used to house a tailor's and now held a vape shop told him he had the right street. As he drove up, his heart sank. The little row of terraced houses that had been converted into bedsits was long gone. A soulless red-brick block sat in its place with a ton of cars outside. He supposed this was progress.

To be fair, the bedsit had been pretty ropey. One of the windows never fully shut and the neighbour used to play music at all hours of the day and night. Lorenzo hadn't cared. He had been in his twenties and loving that he had a place to call his own. But he wouldn't be seen dead having a coffee in a place like that these days, never mind staying the night. He had come a long way since those days.

His old home hadn't been his main destination anyway. He parked up and walked in the footsteps of his twenty-seven-year-old self.

Many a time, he, Jonny and Harry had staggered up this street after spending some of their ill-gotten gains in the bars nearby. They'd been untouchable in those days—Lorenzo and Harry had helped Jonny take control of Manchester's criminal underworld. Everyone cowered when Jonny Wellingham's Boys swaggered past—their reputation for swift justice had been earned tenfold.

Lorenzo crossed the road and soon found the path he wanted. It ran up a back alley of the next street. The red brick walls of the terraces hadn't changed. Memories flooded into his mind like a tsunami.

At the end of the alley, he came to a big car park where he and the lads would set up shop every Wednesday. A regular community operation trading out of a clapped-out Volkswagen campervan. The police had never known a thing.

At the weekends, they'd only dealt in town. However, Jonny had soon realised that a lot of people liked to have their drugs before a night out. So, he would arrange for the van to be in this out-of-the-way spot and punters would come under cover of darkness to do their shopping. One man exclaimed they could only do better if they had a reward points system.

For a moment, Jonny had actually considered it.

A number of public pathways led off the car park. They followed a network of man-made waterways that had been dug to save the area from flooding. As a by-product, they had also created a thriving nature reserve. City dwellers, starved of green space, used them for cycling, jogging and dog walking.

The area had been gentrified since Lorenzo's day. When he had been here, these walkways were the domain of alcoholics and working girls whose customers didn't mind a bunk up against a tree. It was hilarious to him that the middle classes now brought their kids here to study wildlife.

Lorenzo hadn't come here to see insects or birds today. He could remember running through the car park as though the devil himself were after him. Tracing his previous footsteps, knowing what had awaited him that night, sent chills across his skin.

There had been few times in his life when he had experienced real terror. That night, fifteen years ago, still haunted his nightmares.

He'd been watching television in his little flat when they'd burst through the door. Two of them had grabbed his arms while Frank, one of Jonny's lads, had walked up to him.

Lorenzo and Frank had always got on well. The distress at why they had come to inflict pain on him burnt as hot today as it had then. That was before Lorenzo had learnt that true loyalty was a rare diamond, to be cherished when found.

"Wellingham doesn't like your sort," Frank had sneered, grabbing his face. "Shirt-lifters. Problem for you is, he can't just sack you. That leaves only one way out, Lorenzo."

A flash of metal told him all he needed to know about Frank's intentions. Before he could aim, Lorenzo had broken free and leapt through the downstairs window.

The scars on his calves still told that story. His legs had been burning with pain as he'd run across the tarmac, desperate to get to the darkened paths. His thinking had been that he knew this area well. He hoped his attackers didn't.

Retracing that fateful night, he followed the twists and turns. They seemed so innocent in the cold winter sunlight. He could still remember the taste of metallic dread in his mouth. In those days, Lorenzo had been fast. Yet his pursuers had fanned out so he didn't know which way to turn. Voices sounding from every angle sent him into a whirlpool of fear and confusion.

He rounded a hawthorn bush and stopped in his tracks. The hairs on the back of his neck stood on end. *The little pool where my flight came to an end.* The first bullet hit him like a juggernaut smashing into his shoulder. He'd lost his balance and fallen face down into the pool. The pain had seared through his body like hot knives. Instinctively, he reached up and touched where only a scar remained.

Two more bullets had hit him after that, one puncturing a lung. The other had narrowly missed any organs and gone straight through him. Doctors in his future would tell him how lucky he had been. Lying in that ice cold water, waiting to die, luck hadn't felt very close to him.

He'd silently prayed to God to take him quickly, yet he hadn't lost consciousness. Instead, he'd lain there, as still as possible, while his would-be assassins discussed if they'd killed him or not. Every second, he expected an insurance bullet to blow his brains out.

Then his hopes had soared when he'd thought they might be retreating. He'd barely been able to trust his ears as the sounds of his attackers faded.

Lorenzo crouched down and ran his hands through the water. The silt made it a dirty brown. He could imagine a time it would have been deep red with his blood.

Standing up, he filled his lungs with Manchester air. "I am back," he said out loud.

Seeing the place he'd lain, terrified to even breathe, brought a resolve to him. His body had almost frozen as he lay there, waiting to be sure they had gone. Once he could take no more, he had crawled out of the pool, the blood loss and cold making him limp and unable to get up. Instead, Lorenzo had crawled to the car park. Eventually he had got to the main road and thankfully someone driving past had seen him.

They'd saved his life, and he had no idea who they were. He wished he did. They had gone before the paramedics arrived. He supposed they'd recognised him and wanted nothing more to do with it. He could understand that. A man with three gunshot wounds screamed danger. He'd been lucky they'd even dared make the emergency call.

Today he planned to be the one to make an anonymous call. Adrenaline coursed through his veins as he got out the piece of paper with a number written on it. He'd got it from his nephew's friend. She'd thought he intended to use it to taunt Jonny. In a way he did, although he had a much more important outcome on his mind too.

With a shaking hand, he connected the call.

"Who is this?" came the voice that he hadn't heard in decades yet still seemed so familiar to him. "This is a private number. How did you get it?"

"It's a blast from your past," Lorenzo replied.

"Tell me who you are."

"Meet me at the location I message to you," Lorenzo continued. "And all will be revealed. Come alone if you want me to show myself."

He terminated the call. The fish was on the hook. Now he just had to reel it in.

* * * *

Nerves and excitement surged through his body like a runaway train. In every other part of his life, he held control with a tight fist. No one dared change his toilet detergent without checking with him first. He'd buried his feelings for so many years, opting for meaningless sex and making money. Now he had to face them. Lorenzo prided himself on his reputation of fearing no man. That wasn't the case today.

He walked to the exit of the car park and out onto a little square lined with restaurants and shops. It resembled a set from a sci-fi movie. A huge chrome building dominated the place. It housed a theatre and gallery. When he'd lived here, it had only just opened. Now it presided over an entire entertainment complex.

Salford Quays had certainly changed. The Manchester Ship Canal curled around the buildings full of TV channels and media outlets. What had once been the centre of industry now led the way in technology. He supposed Jonny Wellingham had lapped up all this new media money. They spent big and a lot of them on the product that Wellingham specialised in. He wouldn't take kindly to losing it. The thought made Lorenzo grin.

He strolled along the water's edge, pulling his collar up against the icy wind that blew over the water relentlessly. *I wonder what else has changed in Manchester?* Ever since he'd arrived, he'd spent his time organising things at the farmhouse hideout his nephew, Marco, had set up. He hadn't had much of a chance to seek out his old haunts.

The other side of the theatre lay deserted. It only housed a goods entrance. There was a walkway with benches facing the water. Lorenzo clocked a CCTV camera on the building. It couldn't be more perfect. Quiet enough for privacy but no one would attempt anything here.

Leaning against the iron railing, he stared into the water.

What if he doesn't show?

Before he even thought about the consequences of that, he heard footsteps on the stone staircase he'd just come down. It had to be him.

"So, who the fuck are you then?"

Lorenzo turned, and there he stood. The man he had loved more than anyone in the whole world. The man he'd dreamt about and the man he'd almost been killed for. To have him standing in front of him was more than his heart knew what to do with.

A movie reel of memories spun through his mind at warp speed. So many times, he'd wanted to reach out and tell him everything. His thirst for revenge had always trumped his need for reconciliation.

"Hello, Harry," he said.

Harry frowned. "Do I know you?"

Lorenzo made a face. "I haven't aged that much in fifteen years, have I?"

Still Harry stared as though he'd never set eyes on him before. This moment reminded Lorenzo of being at the top of the rollercoaster. Chaos awaited and there wasn't any other option than to wait for it all to play out. Except these days, he drove the rollercoaster.

"Stop fucking me about," Harry said. "Either tell me who you are or I'm out of here."

Lorenzo walked a little closer. Harry instinctively gripped something in his pocket. Of course, he might have come alone, but he was clearly armed. Harry always had been the more paranoid of the two of them.

Lorenzo had had a cockiness that drove a lot of people mad. That bravado had nearly cost him his life.

"Steady on," Lorenzo said. "I survived one shooting. I might not make it through another."

Realisation dawned on Harry's face. "What...it can't be."

Strolling over to him, Lorenzo stared him in the eye. "Take a good look. Surely you remember this face."

Poor Harry looked like he was about to pass out. He wobbled for a second and Lorenzo ran forward, grabbing him. "Do you need to sit down?" he asked.

Harry just nodded. His breathing came in little gasps for air and his legs shook violently. Lorenzo guided him over to a bench and sat him down. Harry put his head between his legs and for a minute or so, remained stock-still.

Did I overdo the drama? *Imagine if I killed Harry before we've even had a chance to say hello.*

"I'm sorry, I didn't know how else to tell you," Lorenzo said as calmly as he could manage. "I wanted you to see me, otherwise you might not believe it was me."

Eventually, Harry raised his head and just stared at him. "Can it be?"

Lorenzo nodded. "It's me, my love. Back from the dead and so fucking pleased to see you."

About the Author

I have written for as long as I could write. In fact, before, when I would dictate to my auntie. I love to read, and I love to create worlds and characters.

I live in the English countryside. When I'm not writing, I like to get out there and think through the next scenario I'm going to throw my characters into.

Inspiration can be found anywhere, on a train, in a restaurant or in an office. I am always in search of the next character to find love in one of my stories. In a world of apps and online dating, it is important to remember love can be found when you least expect it.

Kristian loves to hear from readers. You can find his contact information, website details and author profile page at https://www.pride-publishing.com

PRIDE
PUBLISHING

www.ingramcontent.com/pod-product-compliance
Lightning Source LLC
LaVergne TN
LVHW091054080826
845145LV00002B/740

* 9 7 8 1 8 0 2 5 0 5 2 4 5 *